JUAN

THE SETTLERS BOOK TWO

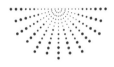

KATHLEEN BALL

Copyright © 2018 by Kathleen Ball

All rights reserved.

No part of this book may be reproduced in any form or by any electronic or mechanical means, including information storage and retrieval systems, without written permission from the author, except for the use of brief quotations in a book review.

❦ Created with Vellum

I dedicate this book to the members of my facebook readers group. Kathleen Ball Western Romance Readers. Thank you for the great input. I appreciate you.

And as always I dedicate this to Bruce, Steven, Colt, Clara, Emery and Mavis because I love them.

CHAPTER ONE

Bone-weary, Juan left the waning daylight behind him and trudged into his house, savoring the peacefulness that surrounded him as he lit a lamp. He was dusty from chasing horses all day and couldn't wait to wash the day's work off. He'd gathered quite a herd so far though, and soon he and his brother Greg would be training them and then selling them to the Cavalry. It felt life changing to have his own place and be starting his own ranch.

A half-eaten loaf of bread sat on his table, and he quickly drew his gun. The loaf had been untouched when he'd left that morning. He turned in a circle, looking for the culprit. No one lived out this far and that was how Juan liked it. He was tired of people staring at him with disdain on their faces because he was Mexican. Under the Oregon law, he was legally considered white, but no one cared about the law. Only about his dark skin.

He relaxed and put his gun back into its holster. No one else was in the small house. Someone had been there, though, and it wasn't the first time. He narrowed his gaze as he took in his surroundings, certain he'd had more cans of beans stacked on the pantry shelf, and his bag of coffee beans seemed lighter than it should be. Someone was stealing from him.

He frowned. He couldn't allow a low-down thief take his things. The fellow needed to work for his food. Juan worked from sun up to sun down to make his way. That was how things were supposed to work. Perhaps he should set a trap. He picked up a knife and sliced up the remaining bread. He had some butter his brother's wife, Mercy had given him, and he spread it on the slices.

After he put the bread on his tin plate, he sat at the wooden table his pa had made. He stopped frowning, thinking of his adopted ma and pa. They'd adopted a whole slew of orphans, including him and his real brother Carlos.

He took another bite of his bread and smiled. Mercy had promised him some blackberry jam soon. He could almost imagine the taste, but she was so busy with her baby Hannah, it might take a while for her to get around to making the sweet treat. Generally he didn't care much for babies, but Hannah had won his heart. She'd been born a bit early and was so tiny that he thought for sure she wouldn't make it. But that little sweetheart had pulled through.

The cry of a child startled him. It was coming from his bedroom. What the heck? He pushed his chair back and rushed toward the cries. He should have checked the bedroom before. The baby stopped its crying. The clink of Juan's spurs and the thud of his feet became the only sound in the room as he strode across the plank floor. His ma would have given him a scowl for keeping them on, but he never took them off in his own house.

He opened the door slowly with his gun in his hand. "Come on out. I know you're in here."

His eyes widened when he saw Sonia Wist step forward with her baby boy. She looked terrified. And she was hurt.

There were bruises on her face and a fresh cut on her bottom lip was bleeding. Her dress had seen better days, and her dark hair had been cut short.

He put his gun away. She looked like a frightened filly that had been beaten. "Hi, Sonia. Come sit at the table and I can make a real dinner."

She shook her head and backed up until her back was against the wall.

"It'll be fine. Besides I bet your boy is hungry." Just then the little boy wailed.

With frantic motions, Sonia tried to get the young child to hush.

"It's going to be just fine, Sonia," Juan said in as comforting a tone as he could muster. "Your baby is hungry. I won't hurt you. I promise."

She stared at him for a long time before she nodded her head and then took a step forward. "I'm—I'm sorry I broke into your home. It's not the first time. Please don't be mad."

He held out his hand to her. "I don't care about missing food. I do care about you and your son. Come, sit down. I'll make you some eggs and then I'll tend to your cuts."

While holding her son in one arm she reached up and touched her lip, wincing. Finally she nodded.

Juan backed up slowly, giving her enough space so she wouldn't feel as nervous. He could see her body shaking. "Here," he said as he pulled out a chair for her. "I'll light the stove. I hope you're not too cold. I didn't think to make a fire for myself, but it is chilly tonight."

Juan walked to the stove and smiled as he heard her sit down. He squatted in front of the cook stove and fiddled with it until it was lit. Maybe he should go and get Mercy to look at Sonia. He bet she had more bruises than were visible.

"I have some milk for the little one. I'm surprised Mercy didn't see you when she left it and the eggs for me. What's his name?" Juan poured milk into a tin cup and put it onto the table.

"Thank you," she whispered. Then she cleared her throat. "His name is Brent."

"That's a fine name. Didn't you marry that Roger fellow?"

"He's dead, and his father came to claim his property. He thought that included me and my son." She kept her gaze on Brent as she gave him small amounts of milk at a time.

"I'm sorry to hear that. How long has your husband been dead?"

"He was shot out of his saddle two months ago. We had a small shack, and his father moved right in the day Roger died."

"That's a tough break. I'm sorry to hear about Roger. What's his father's name?" Juan turned to the stove and fried some eggs along with some bacon.

"Wendell Plank. He doesn't like me very much." The sadness and fear in her voice got to him.

He wasn't sure if he could believe her, though. When she was first pregnant she had tried to claim that his brother Greg was the father. Greg being the good man he was had almost married her. She finally came clean, revealing that the baby's father was a peddler who'd come through town and promised Sonia he'd take her away.

"What about your parents? Won't they help you?"

She hung her head but remained silent.

He put the food on two plates and then placed them on the table; one for him and one for her. "Here we go." Juan sat down, waiting for her to answer him.

"This is very kind of you, Juan," she murmured, pink blooming in her cheeks. "My parents say that I'm dead to them."

He didn't know what to say, so he ate and watched while

she fed Brent the milk and ate too. Soon Brent closed his eyes, and his head flopped against Sonia's shoulder.

"You can put him on my bed if you like. I can put two rolled up blankets on either side of him so he doesn't fall off."

Her surprise pleased him. She almost smiled at him but nodded instead, and then she took Brent into the bedroom.

He breathed a sigh of relief that she was in the other room. What the blazes was he supposed to do with her? It was too dark out to take her to Brian and Mercy's house.

Sonia put Brent on the bed with the two rolled blankets on either side of him. What was to become of her and her son? Her parents suggested she give the baby away and then find a job in the saloon. Tears pricked her eyes at the thought. That was probably her only option now. Well, either that or beg on the streets. She didn't have enough energy left to continue stealing food and sleeping in the barn.

Thank goodness Juan wasn't angry with her. She wouldn't be able to take one more beating from a disgruntled man. Her body ached and she hadn't been able to produce milk for her child. It's a wonder he survived. She wasn't a good mother, she was just all dried up.

She stared down at her baby. He looked more like her than his father, and she was glad. That no good liar deserved to be hanged. He'd probably done this to other girls in the towns he passed through. Now she lived in shame and fear.

Her hands shook, and she clasped them in front of her to stop the movement as she took slow steps out of the bedroom. She closed the door, leaving it cracked open so she could hear if Brent started to fuss. Unsure what to do next, she turned and stared at the floor. The heat of Juan's gaze settled over her, and she couldn't look at him.

"Sonia, take a seat before you fall over," Juan said. His voice had a hard edge to it, and she was sure he wasn't happy that she had stolen from him.

She sat down at the table and finally met his gaze. She expected a glare but instead she thought perhaps he was concerned. He was probably afraid he'd be stuck with her. "We'll be out of here as soon as Brent has slept a bit." It hurt her swollen, split lip to talk.

Without commenting, Juan pushed back his chair and poured some heated water into a small chipped basin. He then grabbed a clean cloth and put it on the table near her. He moved a chair close to her and then he pulled her chair until she was facing him. He sat down and dipped the cloth into the water and then pressed it against her lip.

The sting sharpened but then eased. Startled, she turned her head away.

"It's all right." His voice actually gentled for a moment. "Let's get you cleaned up. This looks fresh." His brow went up.

"I…I went to my parents over a week ago, and they sent me away. I came here, and the house was empty so I stayed inside for three days. I was afraid whoever lived here would catch me. I went back to Wendell's place, and this time he smacked me around and threatened to kill Brent if I didn't, if I… well what he wanted…" She paused for a moment. "Anyway, I had to crawl out of the bedroom window with Brent and I wasn't able to pack my things. All I had packed was a small bag of nappies and clothes for Brent."

He pressed the wet cloth against her lip again. It hurt but she held still. It needed to be cleaned.

"There, I think I stopped the bleeding for a while at least." His voice seemed gentler, and she stared at him. His black hair reached beyond his collar, and his eyes were the deepest shade of brown she'd ever seen. His skin had a tinge of brown to it.

"You're Mexican."

Juan sat back in his chair and his disgust was evident in his scowl. "If you don't want me to touch you, just say so. Are my hands too brown for you? Perhaps you don't want to be in the same room as a Mexican. How didn't you know before?"

Closing her eyes she drew in a deep breath and let it out. She opened them and met his gaze. "I was actually admiring your deep brown eyes and your black hair. It just popped out of my mouth. It's one of my greatest faults. I speak before I think. I do know you're Mexican. You and your brother Carlos. I didn't mean to offend you."

It was silent in the cabin for a bit until he finally nodded his head. "Your parents wouldn't allow me and my brother into the store. We didn't go to town much. I still don't. I'm never comfortable with the stares and whispers."

"I can't say I blame you. I know how it feels. But I want you to know I'll go in the morning."

He sighed. "Where are you planning to go? I don't see as there are too many options out there."

"I don't know but getting away from this town might be good or maybe I could be a mail order bride. Or, well there's always the saloon." She couldn't bring herself to look at him. He'd probably have a look of disgust on his face, and she just couldn't bear to see that.

She bowed her head and stared at her hands. "I was raised in the church, and I tried to be good and follow the teachings, but I went astray. My ma warned me from when I was a little girl that purity was a valued virtue. But when Arthur Spade drove his peddler's wagon into town I was smitten. Then he smiled at me and winked. He paid a lot of attention to me, and he made me feel special. All thought about my future went right out of my head, and when he asked me to sneak out of the house one night I foolishly did as he bade. He was in town for about a week." A tear spilled down her face. "He made me so many promises. We were going to get married and he was going to take me away. One morning, I sat at the breakfast table and learned from my parents that he'd left."

"I'm sorry he led you to believe he cared for you."

His voice held so much compassion she had to lift her head and glance at him. Gone was the hard-edged man. "It's my own fault, and since then all I feel is shame."

Juan tilted his head and stared at her. "Even when you married Roger?"

Warmth filled her face, and she could only imagine how red she had become. "He was paid to marry me. I was lucky he went and got the doctor to help when I was giving birth. He ignored me unless he was drunk. He had a fondness for liquor, and he wasn't the nicest man when he drank. He told me I ruined his life, and he'd have to have more money."

"That must have been tough."

Blinking back tears, she nodded as a lump formed in her throat. "I went and asked my folks for money, and my pa backhanded me and pushed me out of the house." Standing, she gave him a nod. "I think maybe it would be best if Brent and I slept out in your barn. I don't want to cause you any trouble. Like I said, we'll be gone in the morning." She turned and went into the bedroom. Brent was just stirring, and she swept him up into her arms, holding him close. Her soul was in tatters having told Juan all her secrets. What he must think!

She walked out of the bedroom. "If we could just borrow a blanket, I'd be appreciative."

Juan stood and approached her. She cringed and braced for a blow...or worse. Men weren't to be trusted.

"You two take the bedroom; I'll sleep out here in front of the stove. Leave the door open a bit so some of the warmth can get in there."

She stepped back, shaking her head. "I can't do that. I can't leave the door open. I know I must trust you a bit, and I did tell you my problems, but I'm just scared, so scared of what can happen in the dark. That's how it starts, you know. Men have no problem being wicked at night doing things they know they shouldn't and then once they feel comfortable enough they start to do whatever they want whenever they want." She almost made it to the door before Juan stepped in front of her.

"I'll sleep in the barn. You can lock the front door. I understand the need to feel safe."

Before she could say a word, he grabbed his coat and went out the door. "Don't forget to lock the door," he called out.

Sonia locked it and checked it and then checked it again. She put Brent back down on the bed and then she sat in a chair near the warm stove. Her body shook, and she couldn't get it to stop. She liked Juan, he was a nice man, but she was a ruined woman. The sooner she left the better.

A CHILL HUNG on the air the following morning. Juan jammed his hands in his pockets as he paced in front of his door. Were they up yet? He'd hate to wake them, even though he certainly hadn't gotten much sleep. He'd spent the night feeling bad for Sonia. She was a nice person who had made an error in judgement. It was a shame that one indiscretion could leave her life in shambles.

She'd probably be glad to leave his house, though. No white woman wanted a Mexican man. He was always looked at with distrust, sometimes with outright malice. He couldn't change things. It was safer for him to stay on the ranch.

Without warning, the door opened and he smiled at Sonia as she hovered just on the other side of the threshold. She gave him a slight smile back. The circle under her eyes told a story of a sleepless night.

"Good morning, Juan. Would you like breakfast? I could make you some."

Without giving her an answer, he walked into his cabin and put more wood in the cook stove.

"I bet you just want to get on with your day…" She drew a deep breath and added, "I hope you don't mind if I borrow one of your blankets to wrap Brent in."

"You can take whatever you need."

She gave him a quick nod and bundled Brent up. Head held high, she left.

Part of him wanted to run after her, but it would only lead to trouble. If people knew she'd been here they were sure to be outraged. She might not have a good reputation but she was still white. He should have let her make and eat breakfast, though. Had Brent had his milk? An ache throbbed in Juan's heart. He just felt sorry for her. That was all it was.

He sat down and pounded his fist on the table. Why hadn't he taken her to his parents' house? They would have known what to do with her.

After a soft knock on the door, it opened and in stepped Mercy, his brother Greg's wife. She had the blondest hair he'd ever seen, and she could out rope half the men on the ranch.

She smiled. "I baked too many loaves of bread again." She laid two fresh loaves on the table. "I saw all the horses in the corral. You should have seen how excited Greg was last night when he saw them. I'd best get back, he's watching Hannah, and I might get back to find he tried to feed her pancakes. I

JUAN

keep telling him he has to wait until her teeth come in." She stopped talking and stared at Juan. "What's wrong?"

"I came home to find food missing, and I found Sonia and her baby here." He shrugged. "I fed them and let them sleep here last night while I slept in the barn. She's had a hard time of it, and I just let her walk out this morning with nothing more than a blanket to keep the baby warm. I feel bad." He stood and went to the window and stared out at the swaying long grass. "I wish I could have gone after her."

"What about her husband?"

"He was shot dead, and then his father moved in. You should have seen the split lip she had and the bruises. Her parents refuse to take her in." He ran his fingers through his hair. "I should have made her stay, but all I could think about was the trouble it would bring if she was found here. I'd be strung up so fast..." He turned and saw the understanding in Mercy's eyes.

"How long ago did she leave?"

"Not too long before you got here."

Mercy smiled and shook her head. "What are you waiting for? Go get her. And bring her and the baby to your ma. She'll figure something out for the two of them."

He put on his gun belt and smashed his hat on his head. "I'm riding out. Tell Greg I'll be back in a while. He can have fun looking over the horses. And Mercy, thank you." He walked to her and kissed her on the cheek before he left.

Sonia hadn't gotten far. He found her down the dusty dirt road sitting on a rock trying to sooth a screaming Brent. His gut clenched as he got nearer to her. The short curls of her molasses colored hair were blowing back and forth as the wind gusted. Why had she cut it? It was odd, he'd never seen a woman with short hair before.

He reined in Journey, his gelded paint, and then slid off the horse. At the last minute, he remembered his manners and snatched off his hat, and then he smiled at her. It probably wasn't much of a smile since he didn't have anything happy to smile about.

"Juan, you caught me resting instead of walking." She stood, still trying to quiet Brent by rubbing his back as she held him to her.

"I was looking for you. You two can't be wandering around with nowhere to go. I'm taking you to my ma. She'll know what to do."

Sonia shook her head. "She'll want Brent but not me. I've become an undesirable person since my downfall. I can't taint her reputation by asking for her help."

In that moment, he felt her pain of rejection. It was a feeling he was well acquainted with. "She can at least tell us where to go." He tilted his head as he stared at her while she looked out over the landscape of hills and trees.

She sucked on her lip for a minute. Just as he thought she wasn't going to answer, she spoke. "I'll go with you, but I want you to ask her permission for me to be there before I talk to her." Her voice wobbled.

She startled as he picked her up, baby and all, and placed her on the horse. Then he jumped on behind her. Grabbing the reins, he had her in his arms. Before urging Journey to move, he patted Brent on the back and was surprised when the child stopped crying.

This time his smile was real when Sonia gave him a sidelong look. He spurred Journey on and they were at the big house in no time. He was almost reluctant to jump down. It meant he'd have to remove his arms from Sonia and Brent. He carefully lifted them down, and if there hadn't been an audience he'd have held her a bit longer.

Hunter and Carlos were there to greet them.

"Will you keep Sonia and Brent company while I talk to

Ma?" He didn't wait for their response; he knew they'd do as he asked.

He climbed the few steps to the porch and walked into the house. His ma was sitting in the rocking chair holding Rose.

The sweet smile he'd grown to appreciate lit her face. He remembered that same smile when he and Carlos had just lost their parents and they'd been left at a fort along the Oregon Trail. No one wanted them, and the man who ran the fort, a man named Bridger, was set to put them out. She was like an angel, swooping in and gathering them both into her arms.

The next thing he knew he and Carlos were part of a big family of orphans. Their pa taught them to love one another as siblings should. His pa was a special man who raised three other brothers on his own. The brothers Mike, Eli, and Jed had families now, but they'd all combined land and now they had a huge spread. They didn't have to give him his own section to raise horses but they had.

"I'd give you a big hug and kiss," his ma murmured. "But Rose didn't sleep well last night and well, she's finally asleep. I'm almost afraid to put her down lest she wake."

"I need to talk to you. You remember Sonia Wist, don't you?"

"Yes, I do. She claimed that Greg fathered her baby." She shook her head.

"I have her with me. Please, Ma, listen before you answer." He waited for her nod before continuing. "She married Roger Plank, and he died a few months back. Now Roger's father has moved in with her and her son. Ma, she has a split lip and her face is bruised. I can only imagine how many other bruises she may have. She left and went to her parents who told her to go away. She'd been staying at my place while I was rounding up horses. I don't know what to do with her. She left this morning, but I knew she had nowhere to go, so I went after her and she's outside. She didn't want to come in until you gave your permission. She didn't want to ruin your good name by associating with her. She has her baby with her, Ma."

"Here, take Rose and put her in the cradle. Don't wake her," she whispered.

He gently took Rose and put her into her wooden cradle without her waking.

"Come on," his ma said as she took his hand in hers. "If she matters to you, she matters to me, Juan. Let's go and invite her inside."

Relief coursed through him at her words. He gave her hand a quick squeeze before he let go, and then he held the door open for her when they went outside.

The look of fear in Sonia's eyes touched him and angered him. He'd like to go beat Wendell Plank, but he'd be sure to be strung up for it. It had taken a lot of practice to learn to remain calm in public.

His ma put her arms around Sonia, and the tears in Sonia's eyes made him hurt inside.

"I'm Lynn, Sonia. Welcome. I hear you're having a hard time. Let's go inside and get you and your boy something to eat, and then we'll talk. I'm sorry for the way things turned out for the both of you."

"Oh boy, she's a crier," Carlos groaned. Juan chuckled as he went inside. Carlos had a lot to learn.

CHAPTER TWO

Sonia looked around as she entered the large house. It appeared bigger than it looked from outside. There was nothing fancy about it, but it looked homey and inviting, with patterned quilts hanging on the walls. There were numerous chairs circled in front of the massive rock fireplace. Glancing at the kitchen, her jaw almost opened. There were two cook stoves, and the dining table was the longest she'd ever seen.

"Can I get you a cup of tea?" Lynn asked as she gestured for Sonia and Brent to sit down in front of the fireplace. "Juan, could you move the coffee table in front of the chair Sonia is going to sit in?"

Without a word Juan lifted the square table and set it so Sonia would have a place to put her tea. When he was done, he laid his hand on her shoulder and gave her an encouraging squeeze. Looking up, she met his gaze and nodded. She could do this despite her stomach filling with butterflies. Lynn would probably give her a few words of wisdom and send her on her way.

Lynn and Smitty Settler had a houseful. There probably

wasn't room for her. She glanced at the baby girl sleeping peacefully and her eyes widened at the sight of two more cradles, both empty.

Sonia swallowed hard as waves of longing washed over her. They wouldn't want someone with her reputation tainting their good home. She'd enjoy the tea and go on her way.

Lynn came back with a tray holding a teapot and three cups. She placed the tray on the table and handed Juan a cup. "Coffee for you, Juan. I know how much you hate tea."

There was love in Juan's eyes as he smiled at his mother. He was a good man. If he cared for his ma that much, imagine how much love he had to give a wife and children.

Brent began to fuss, and he didn't seem to want to be comforted by her. The heat spreading over her face just made it worse, and her frustration brought on jerky movements as she tried to pat his back. What kind of mother couldn't quiet her own child?

"What's his name?" asked Lynn softly.

"Brent. He's almost seventeen months old."

"He's not walking yet? Does he talk at all?" Lynn held out her arms. "Here, let me hold him."

After a moment's hesitation, Sonia gave her son over to Lynn and was surprised how quiet he became.

Lynn looked Brent over and then sat in a rocking chair and rubbed his back as she held him against her shoulder. After a short time, she glanced up. "He's sleeping." She stood and carried him over to one of the empty cradles and set him down. The she covered him with a baby blanket.

"What's your trick, Ma?" Juan asked.

"Babies can tell if you're nervous, and then it's hard for them to settle down. Happens a lot with new mothers." Lynn poured the tea and handed Sonia a cup. "Do you want sugar or milk in it?"

"No, thank you this is lovely."

Lynn sat back down and smiled. "First of all, Brent is adorable, but he should be babbling and perhaps talking by now. Just a word here and there. I'm also concerned he isn't walking yet. He may be a bit delayed."

Sonia's heart squeezed. She didn't even know when a baby should start walking or talking. "It's all my fault. I didn't know…"

"It's not your fault. Babies teach themselves at first. They crawl then start pulling themselves up and lean against furniture. Soon enough they start to walk. Not all children are the same though. They all learn at a different rate."

"I…I had to keep him in the bedroom whenever Roger was home. Then at night he'd carry the empty drawer I was using as a cradle into the main room. He wanted nothing to do with him. His father Wendell acted pretty much the same. He'd get so mad when Brent would cry. He thought it was my fault. They were both hateful men."

Lynn reached over and gave Sonia's hand a gentle squeeze. "You're safe now." She leaned back in the chair and stared at Juan. "I think the best course of action is to have you live here for a while. But you must take care of Brent yourself. I'm always willing to lend a hand but my hands are pretty full. I think you'll like it here." Lynn gave her a big smile that warmed Sonia's heart.

Relief flooded through her. She had a place to stay for now.

The door opened, and a bunch of noisy kids of all ages pushed through, tumbling and stumbling over one another.

"Hush!" admonished Lynn.

They all fell silent as they stopped and stared at Sonia. There were several new faces in the group, but she'd known a few of them. Many used to stop into her parent's mercantile, but her father had put a stop to it. He'd called them dirty beggars and chased them away. Sonia's face heated at the memory.

"What's she doing here?" Will asked, scowling.

"I would have thought she'd be too ashamed to show her face around here," Scarlett scoffed as she folded her arms in front of herself.

Hunter frowned. "What's going on? Ma, do I need to escort her off the property?"

"Oh, my!" Scarlett exclaimed, pointing at the cradle. "She's leaving her baby here. I knew it. I knew you weren't any good. Greg really got lucky when he didn't marry you." Scarlett whirled and glared at Sonia.

Lynn stood up. "Keep your voices down. Rose is finally sleeping and so is little Brent. I suggest we all go outside and have a discussion about how rude my children are. Scoot now."

Sonia stayed in her chair. They probably didn't want her out there, and she didn't want to hear what they had to say.

"Sonia," Lynn said gently. "Come on, this concerns you." She waited at the door until Sonia joined her.

Shame and fear filled her, and it took everything she had to follow Lynn outside. Now all the kids were giving her dirty looks.

"I don't want to cause any trouble," she said to Lynn. "I think it best I leave."

"Good idea!" Will shouted.

"Stop it this minute. Sonia needs our help." Lynn shook her head.

Will glowered. "Hunter, I guess you'll have to marry her. When is the baby due?"

Sonia took in a loud sharp breath. "I was just on my way."

Lynn put her arm around Sonia's waist. "I've raised you all better than this. I'm so disappointed in all of you. Sonia needs a place to stay for a while, and I offered to let her stay with us. It's my decision, and you don't get a say. Now I want you all to apologize to Sonia, and I expect better behavior from all of you."

Movement in the corner of her eye caught Sonia's attention. Smitty was walking toward them, and he didn't look happy. "What's this all about?" He stared at Sonia with expressionless eyes.

Lynn let go of Sonia and walked to Smitty's side. "You remember Sonia, don't you?"

"Yes I do." He didn't sound happy either.

"Roger died, and his father moved in, and she has bruises."

Smitty's gaze met Lynn's. "The baby?"

"He's here."

Smitty nodded. "Sonia, come here please."

She shook as she walked to him. The next thing she knew she was in his arms as he hugged her. It was the most soul-healing hug she'd ever gotten, and it saddened her when it ended.

"You're more than welcome to stay with us. I see the bruises now. Why don't you go inside with Lynn so she can doctor you up. Where's your baby?"

"He's inside, Mr. Settler," she answered quietly.

"Call me Smitty. Hunter will do baby duty, Cindy and Mia can cook tonight. Anthony and Jax can do the dishes. Will, I want you to take a walk with me, you too, Scarlett." Smitty's orders weren't questioned.

Sonia was surprised as she watched Cindy and Mia hustle inside while Will and Scarlett walked toward the barn with Smitty. It felt a bit cold without Smitty near. She wouldn't stay too long.

"Come on, Sonia, it'll be fine." Lynn smiled and then she turned and walked into the house.

Sonia hesitated for a moment, but Brent's cry made her decision for her and she quickly went inside. She picked him up and soothed him. It was a relief when he quieted so fast.

Hunter approached her, and she looked into his blue eyes. He looked dependable. He held out his arms and took the baby. He held Brent against his shoulder while he patted the baby's back. "It'll be fine. Go on with, Ma."

Sonia gave him a grateful smile and went up the stairs with Lynn. She was led into a room with four beds, one against each wall. It was a pleasant enough bedroom with colorful quilts on each bed.

Lynn gestured toward the bed against the same wall the door was located in. "This will be yours. We'll carry the cradle up at night so Brent can sleep near you. Then we'll bring it back down in the morning. It seems to work out well enough. Now sit and take off that dress while I gather some supplies and a clean dress for you."

Overwhelmed by Lynn's kindness, Sonia began to shake. To cover it, she nodded and turned away.

With a soft sigh, Lynn turned and left the room.

JUAN'S EYES narrowed as he watched Greg head toward him wearing a big ole grin. That was odd, since his brother saved most of his smiles for Mercy.

Juan turned away and put his foot up on the bottom rung of the wooden fence that made up the horse corral. Greg could grin all he wanted. Juan just didn't want to know.

Greg stood next to him and put his foot on the rung too. "Guess what!"

Juan wanted to groan out loud. "What?"

"You're not going to guess?"

"Nope, and I don't want to know. Unless it has something to do with my niece, Hannah. Otherwise don't tell me."

Greg frowned. "You take the fun out of everything. We've been summoned for supper tonight. Something about meeting your girlfriend." Greg stared at him but he couldn't keep a straight face. "I thought you said you never wanted a girlfriend."

Juan shook his head and scowled. "It's your girlfriend. I'm just being nice."

Greg appeared dumbfounded. "My girlfriend? Those could be considered fightin' words."

This time Juan smiled. It was fun to get Greg riled. "It's Sonia."

"Sonia Wist?" Greg's eyebrows rose. "Thought she married that Roger fella. What happened that you had to be nice? I know it goes against your grain."

Juan grunted. "Roger is six feet under, and his father came to live with Sonia and her baby boy. Seems Wendell can't keep himself from hitting her." Juan turned until he faced Greg. "Her parents disowned her, and she'd been staying at my place on and off while I was away catching horses. She didn't even have a coat to wear."

"The baby?"

"Cute little thing. He looked well. She named him Brent. I didn't know what to do with her so I took her to Ma. That's the reason for the summons, I figure."

"Ohh, she's your problem now. Well that's good. I don't think Mercy would like it if I brought another woman home."

"It's not like that. Hell, you almost married her when she was pregnant."

Greg grimaced. "True enough. I missed that bullet. What do you plan to do with her?"

Juan shrugged. "Like I said, I gave her to Ma. She's not my problem."

Greg nodded. "I'm going to get cleaned up for supper. Do you want to wait for us or are you going alone?"

Juan laughed. "You and Mercy take forever, and I don't think it's getting ready that takes so much time. I'll meet you there. And Greg? Take it easy on Sonia. She looks like she was beaten, and her clothes were torn."

"I'll behave. See ya later."

Juan stood watching the horses. Most looked promising but a few wouldn't be sold to the Army. The Army only wanted the best and he and Greg needed to make a name for themselves if they planned to train horses for the long term.

He went into the house, washed and put on a clean shirt. Hopefully, Sonia had made friends with his sisters; though Scarlett could be a bit prickly at times. Ma would take good care of her and the baby. Tomorrow he'd pay Wendell a visit and explain to him that men didn't beat women.

He went out to the barn and saddled Journey. The horse reminded Juan of himself; part brown and part white. He mounted up and made the short ride to the big house.

He slid off Journey's back, took his time removing the saddle, and then let the paint go out to the pasture. He turned and studied the house. There was a lot of love inside, and usually he enjoyed having supper with his huge family, but tonight his stomach was tied up in knots. Did the others think that Sonia was his girl? Sighing, he walked to the door and pushed it open.

It was hectic and noisy with a few of his siblings fighting and the little ones running around. He closed the door behind him and couldn't help but scan for Sonia. He finally saw her holding a fussing Brent. Juan walked by everyone and took the baby from her. Brent smiled and put his head on Juan's shoulder.

The house became mostly silent, and he knew what he'd just done. His heart sank as he turned toward his family. He'd just laid claim to Sonia. How stupid could he be? Maybe Hunter could take her off his hands. He was old enough.

Everyone smiled at him, and he wanted to swear but there was no swearing allowed in the house or around the kids. He'd done it now; he'd have to fix it later. He glanced down at Sonia, pleasantly surprised at how she glowed. Her short dark hair curled around her face and looked quite becoming. The yellow dress she wore looked nice on her too, but it was her shining blue eyes that got to him. She looked happy to see him.

"You look well," he told her.

She nodded as she continued to stare at him. "Brent is fond of you."

"All babies like me. I don't know why exactly, but they do. How was your day? Did you get to meet everyone?"

She blushed under his scrutiny. "Yes, everyone has been more than cordial to me. You have a wonderful family."

"Greg and Mercy should be here soon," his ma announced to the hungry crowd.

He laughed at the groans and Sonia looked up at him.

"They're always late," Juan explained.

"Very late," added nine-year-old Cotton. "They like to kiss and stuff, and we end up waiting."

Sonia turned even redder than before, but she made no comment.

"Cotton, we don't gossip," Lynn said gently. "But you do have a point, we're all so hungry. Why don't we sit down and eat."

Juan hung back with Sonia while a younger child sat next to an older one. Lynn sat at one end while Smitty took the seat at the other.

"There's room next to me," Carlos called out to Juan.

Juan nodded and placed his hand on the small of Sonia's back, walking her over to the bench. He still held Brent as he sat next to Carlos. Sonia settled next to Juan.

"Here, I can take Brent. It'll make it easier for you to eat. He's been fed so don't worry about trying to get him to eat."

Juan started to hand Brent to her when Brent screeched piercingly. He continued to scream despite all of Sonia's attempts to calm him. She started to get up from the table.

"Give him here," Juan said, reaching for the child.

She shook her head. "I'll just take him upstairs so everyone can eat in peace."

Juan continued to hold out his arms, and Brent wriggled and reached toward Juan as though he was his lifesaver. As soon as Brent was in Juan's arms, he laid his head back on Juan's shoulder and after a few shaky breaths; he made a sound of contentment.

Pa smiled and said grace. Juan couldn't help but feel his approval and it fixed a part of his heart he hadn't realized was broken. Juan glanced at Carlos, who scowled and shook his head.

"You'd make a good nanny, Juan," Carlos said, his words dripped with sarcasm.

"I don't know much about little kids," Juan said with a shrug. "But I did have to hold you a lot. I'm surprised I'm not half deaf with all the screaming and crying you used to do."

Crimson crept into Carlos' face and he glowered at Juan in anger.

"Of course you cried because we didn't have much food," admitted Juan.

Carlos' shoulders relaxed, and he nodded. "Well, we have plenty now."

Juan gave him a smile. "Yes, we are blessed."

The bowls and platters of food were passed around, and Sonia served both herself and Juan. She was a caring person, who was just down on her luck. Juan scanned the faces of everyone at the table, realizing that most of them had been in the same situation at one point or another.

"This is very good," Sonia complimented.

"Thank you," Cindy and Mia both said in unison.

Sonia then cut up the food on Juan's plate and fed him while he held Brent. It was embarrassing to be fed like a child, but there was something tender to it too. Their gazes met and held with each forkful.

The door opened, admitting Greg, Mercy, and Hannah. Ma got up right away and took Hannah in her arms. "I love having grandbabies." She started for her rocking chair but stopped and turned around. "Hello Greg, hello Mercy, you'd have thought I was raised without manners."

Pa laughed. "We forgive you when babies are concerned." They exchanged a loving look before Ma went to sit in her chair.

"See I told you they'd be late," Cotton announced.

"What's the excuse this time? Were you kissing again?" Will asked.

Pink bloomed in Mercy's cheeks as her jaw dropped open. Greg gave each of the boys a glare before he led Mercy to a seat.

"If you must know, Mercy changed her dress three times. I think I liked it better when she had no dresses," Greg teased.

"It's good to see you again, Sonia. This is Mercy, my wife, and Ma is holding our daughter Hannah," Greg said, and his voice sounded sincere.

"It's nice to see you too, Greg. Mercy, I hope we get a chance to get to know one another," Sonia replied. Her body shook a bit, and Juan took her hand in his.

"Who do you have there, Juan?" Mercy asked.

"Mercy's son, Brent. They'll be staying here for a bit."

Mercy smiled at Sonia. "It's such a loving place to be. I'm sure you'll enjoy it."

"Thank you. I'm sure I will enjoy it for the short time I'll be here."

Juan squeezed her hand until she looked at him.

"A-actually, I don't know how long I'll be here," she stammered. "I'm sure I'll find a place to live somewhere, but it's hard to find work with a little one."

"What about getting married again? There's going to be a party here on Friday. We can start looking for a prospective husband for you." Mercy smiled, seeming excited.

Sonia pulled her hand from Juan's grasp. "I don't know if I'll ever marry again. It's preferable to be alone, with Brent of course."

"Mia made apple pies for us," Pa said. "I know I'd love a piece."

Mia beamed happily. "I'll dish them up."

"The dress you're wearing looks nice on you," Juan whispered to Sonia. She ducked her head and looked at her hands that were folded in her lap. She was nothing like the spoiled girl she used to be, and he was glad.

Brent was now wide awake and he studied and touched every part of Juan's face. The small boy didn't know what gentle meant. He tugged at Juan's nose and lips and then dug both hands into Juan's hair and refused to let go. There was much laughter around the table and he felt deep down that things would work out. Sonia would be happy living with his ma and pa.

"Do you want to go see a horsey?" he asked the boy.

The boy nodded vigorously.

"Does that mean yes?" Juan asked patiently.

"Papa," Brent replied looking solemn. Then he smiled as if pleased with himself.

Juan glanced at Sonia, and there were tears in her eyes. "Come on, Sonia, you can see the horsies too."

They left the table and went out into the chilly air left behind by the setting sun. The barn wasn't as far from the house, and they quickly walked across they yard. It was dark inside and when Juan tried to give Brent to Sonia so he could light the lamp, Brent squealed. Sonia lit the lamp instead. It gave off a soft glow that enhanced her beauty. When had he started thinking of her as beautiful?

Juan stopped in front of a stall, and a dainty mare poked her nose out. "Brent, this is Milly."

Brent tried to lunge for the horse, but she didn't move, she just watched.

"Brent, you need to stay still," Sonia said, worry straining her voice.

"It's fine. Milly, here, is the horse that all the kids meet first. She's a gentle soul."

She hesitated a few seconds. "If you're sure."

He smiled. "It'll be fine."

"Brent, see how big the horse is?"

Brent made a noise and wiggled his fingers toward Milly.

"She has soft fur, but you have to pet the horse not pull it's hair. Let me show you."

Juan stroked Milly's face. "See? It looks like she's smiling. Would you like to try?"

Brent stared with wide eyes and then nodded.

"Yes?"

"Yesh," Brent said clearly.

Juan had a good hold on the boy, prepared for him to pull at Milly's fur, but to his surprise he gently petted the mare, his lips curving upward in obvious delight. He'd never really seen Brent smile before. The child turned and petted Juan's face and giggled. "Papa, horshey."

Juan laughed. "Oh yeah? You think I'm a horsey?"

Brent nodded and patted Juan's face again.

"Give Milly a pat good night. It way past her bedtime."

Brent turned back to Milly and petted her face, and Juan was able to easily move Brent away when he went to pull her ears. When he turned, he saw the tears in Sonia's eyes.

"Hey, what's wrong?"

"He's talking. He never talked before, and I'm so sorry he's calling you Papa. It must be embarrassing for you." A tear trailed down her face.

"Don't worry about it, Sonia. He'll call whoever you marry Papa. He did say horsey though. Mighty smart boy you have here," he commented before he tickled the boy's stomach. After he walked them back to the house, he said good bye to his family and rode home.

He didn't know why his emotions were all over the place. He usually split his time between two emotions: anger and love for his family. It was something different with Sonia and Brent, and it disturbed him. He liked his solitary life.

CHAPTER THREE

*B*rent was fussing so Sonia slipped out of bed and carried him downstairs. It wouldn't do for him to wake the other girls. It was cold so she stoked the cook stove and added some wood to it. She put on some coffee to boil and then sat in a rocking chair with Brent.

He'd had men in his life, not good men, but he decided to call Juan "Papa." It frightened her. They probably thought she'd taught him to call Juan that. She kissed the top of Brent's dark hair. The main thing was he did talk. He was contentedly babbling to her now, looking very pleased with himself.

Just the short time he'd spent watching the other children had been good for him. But now what? She couldn't stay here very long. She'd have to keep an open mind at the party on Friday. Maybe she could find a husband. It would have to be someone who was new to the area. Her dirty laundry had been aired by all in town a few years ago.

Reaching up, she touched her short hair. Roger had done it to shame her. He'd known she was with child before he married her, but he acted as though she'd cheated on him and insisted she wear her hair short to remind her of her sins. It was always the one who didn't go to church that called others sinners. Her parents had made her kneel on grains of rice for hours to help her repent for her sin. They did go to church, but it was more for the social aspect than to praise God.

People looked at her hair oddly, but no one ever asked. Roger had taken a knife and chopped off her hair, and it had been so painful. He told her that all men would know she was a fallen woman just by looking at her. It was a wonder that Brent survived it all and came out perfect.

She'd been relieved when she saw her husband's dead body, but suddenly his father showed up. Roger must have learned his abusive ways from his father. It was a nightmare from the start, but she didn't think herself strong enough to leave. Plus Wendell promised to kill Brent if she tried to escape.

It had taken all of her courage to run when she did. It was stupid, with nowhere to go. But for now they were safe, and she was grateful. Very grateful. Yes, she'd find someone on Friday. Perhaps Scarlett could give her pointers on how to dress and act.

Smitty was the first one to come down the stairs. "Good morning. Looks like you did my job for me."

"Brent was fussing so I brought him down here." There was something about Smitty that made her feel as though everything would be fine. Lynn was a lucky woman.

"Lynn will be down in a few minutes. Are you ready for tonight?"

She furrowed her brow. "Tonight?"

"We're having a party. It's to celebrate Lynn and me being married for two years now. She invited almost the whole town. It'll be a busy day. Don't worry if you don't feel up to help with the preparations. I want you to enjoy the party." His eyes were full of happiness, and that made her wistful.

"I'll do what I can."

"How'd you sleep? Lynn asked as she entered the room. She bent and gave Smitty a kiss on his cheek.

"Fine until early this morning, when Brent started to fuss."

"Kids are good at that." She poured three cups of coffee and handed then out. "I heard Brent call Juan, Papa."

Sonia's stomach clenched, and her heart pounded painfully against her chest. "Yes, yes he did. I didn't tell him to or anything. I mean I don't—"

Lynn put a comforting hand on Sonia's shoulder. "It's great he started to talk is all I meant. Juan couldn't wait to be on his own, but personally I think he's a bit lonely."

Smitty laughed. "You wouldn't be trying to play matchmaker, would you?"

Lynn winked at him. "Of course not. Besides, you might find a beau at the party. Amos Shepard is bringing over a pig to roast, and everyone else is bringing a dish to pass."

"Happy anniversary," Sonia said trying not to turn red from the talk about beaus. It was awkward to say the least but Lynn was right, she needed to find someone to take her in. "What can I do to help?"

"I'll need someone to put the pieces of cloth on the tables and pick some flowers to put in the middle of the tables. We'll get started right after breakfast. People will be arriving around two, I believe," Lynn said happily.

TWO O'CLOCK CAME TOO FAST for Sonia. Her nerves were stretched so taut, Brent wouldn't relax. He wore the cutest outfit of navy blue short pants with a blue shirt that Lynn had laid out for him. Scarlett had been reluctant at first to help Sonia, but after a fashion, she loaned her a beautiful lavender dress with a bit of lace on it. Sonia had almost cried. She hadn't worn anything so nice since she was a young girl living with her parents.

Now she stood outside worrying. She was bound to be the object of gossip.

"Sonia," Lynn said in her gentle tones. "Why don't you take this quilt and spread it under that tree and let Brent try to crawl. He might not fuss as much."

Sonia took the quilt and smiled. "Thank you. I'm so nervous."

Lynn patted her hand. "You look lovely. Just enjoy yourself."

Sonia gave her a smile before she walked to the tree. It was the perfect place. There was shade and she wasn't in the middle of where people would be gathered. If she was lucky, people wouldn't pay her much attention. As soon as she spread out the quilt, she placed Brent on it. She put him face-down to see if he would indeed try to crawl.

He pushed his arms up and laughed. It took him a few attempts, and he tipped over several times, but her heart almost burst watching him crawl awkwardly across the quilt. He was so busy he didn't fuss at all. He'd made strides in just a few days. She'd never dared to put him on the floor before. Without a doubt, Roger would have stepped on him, or worse.

She was happy watching him explore and had picked him up to turn his direction so many times, she didn't realize just how many people had arrived. Tables were laden with food and people were having a good time, laughing and talking to each other. Loneliness grabbed at her and wouldn't let go. She wasn't a part of their society, not a welcome one. For a moment, she couldn't breathe, and her eyes watered. Finally anger took over. She'd been friends with those same people until they turned their backs on her.

Well, she'd be fine just watching from the quilt. Her only problem would be to get Brent some food. Maybe one of the Settlers would check on her. Scarlett was the belle of the party. All the young men flocked to her. Mia stood by with a jealous look on her face. Jealousy was indeed ugly.

Hunter looked busy getting punch for the young ladies, while Carlos and Anthony stared at the pretty girls. In a few years, they'd have their turn wooing all the females. It looked like an exciting time in a young person's life. Sonia sighed. She'd thrown it all away. Now she was just an unwanted bystander.

She reached out and hugged Brent. He was worth it all.

A shadow fell over them and she glanced up, hoping it was Juan, but it was a few of the girls she'd gone to school with. She nodded at them and promptly ignored them.

"I can't believe you'd cart your shame in public. That baby is a bastard," Tricia said as she put her hands on her hips and scowled.

Sonia had never noticed just how ugly Tricia really was, and to think she'd called her friend. The other two, Missy and Kimberly, stared at her with ugly frowns on their faces.

"I think you'd best go back to where you came from," Missy said. "The Settlers are good people, and they don't want your kind here."

"My kind?" She shouldn't have asked.

Kimberly stepped forward and her perfect blond curls bounced becomingly. "You know, the kind of woman who is a whore. You didn't even know that peddler, yet you lay with him. Then you blamed Greg Settler for getting you with child. You're a disgrace! Even your own kin don't want you around. So go back to that shack you live in and let the good people enjoy themselves."

Sonia was afraid they'd actually spit on her. She pulled Brent against her and turned her head away. They weren't saying anything that wasn't true. "I'd leave you be, but I'm staying here now."

Tricia narrowed her eyes. "You were always such a liar!"

"Ladies I'm going to have to ask you to leave if you continue to insult one of my guests," Greg Settler practically growled.

Sonia looked up at Greg and saw Juan coming their way. From his compressed lips and his stormy glare, he was furious. Greg put his hands on Juan's shoulders to keep him from pouncing on the girls.

Hunter joined the group, looking very handsome in his good clothes. His chocolate brown hair curled around his collar, and his eyes matched the color of the sky. He walked around the women and sat down next to Sonia.

"Sonia is a friend of the family, so unless you're here to make pleasant conversation, I'd appreciate it if you went and got yourself some punch or something."

Missy, Tricia, and Kimberly turned and started to walk away, and Sonia heard them say something about her fooling all the Settler men.

"Thank you, Hunter. Thank you Greg and Juan too. If I'd been alone it would have been fine but my son is with me." She sighed heavily. "You can all go back to the party."

Juan opened his mouth, but Hunter spoke first. "I'll stay and keep you company."

Greg and Juan glanced at each other.

Juan narrowed his eyes as he looked at Hunter. "Keep her safe."

Hunter only nodded.

Juan's face softened when he stared at her. "I'll be by in a bit to visit with you."

She watched as the two brothers walked away.

"He has it bad for you," Hunter said, grinning. "Juan doesn't take to many people but he sure likes you."

"He just feels responsible for me since I was hiding in his house is all. He's a good man, and he's so good with Brent."

Hunter nodded. "You do know that if you marry him, you'll have a hard life, don't you?"

"What do you mean?" She had an idea of what he was going to say.

"He's Mexican. There are some in the community that won't do business with him. I know your parents banned him and Carlos from their store. I see his struggle to keep his temper in check, but one of these days I think he'll explode."

She put Brent back down and watched him crawl. "No one will receive me in their establishments either. Juan doesn't want a woman in his life. He's a loner and happy to be one."

Hunter reached out and turned Brent so he could crawl toward his mother. "You're right about that, but I see the way he looks at you. I'm sorry you've been made to suffer with your dead husband. I never thought much of Roger, but I didn't know he beat women."

"Water under the bridge." She shrugged and pushed a smile to her lips. "I need to plan a future for me and Brent. I never want to marry again, but there aren't many choices for a woman with a child. I just want to enjoy the day. I don't have the luxury of knowing I'll have food for the both of us very often."

Hunter smiled. "Ma takes good care of us all. Pa too."

She smiled back. "They are such a loving couple. I'm glad they found each other."

Her mood grew brighter when she spotted Juan walking in her direction with a plate of food. Brent had just made it to her, and she laughed. "You little stinker. He's learning so much so fast."

Brent clapped and yelled "Papa!" when he saw Juan approaching. A longing filled with love exploded inside Juan, and he didn't know what to do. He handed the plate to Sonia and lifted Brent up into his arms. The boy snuggled against him and sighed contently. He then stared at Juan's face. "Papa!" he crowed.

Juan laughed. "I've watched you crawling around like a big boy."

Brent nodded happily, and when Juan tried to put him down he held on tight. He wasn't about to be set down unless Juan pried his fists open.

"Aren't you hungry?" Juan asked him.

"Food."

"Yes, very good. That is food. Don't you want some?"

Brent shook his head. "Papa..." Smacking his lips, Brent pointed to himself.

"Kiss?"

"Kish." Again he smacked his lips and then he touched his cheek.

Juan kissed Brent's cheek with a loud smacking noise. Brent laughed and allowed himself to be put down.

"I can take it from here, Hunter. Go and find yourself a young lady to dance with," Juan said.

"Why? Is Sonia taken?" Hunter teased, but he quickly got up when Juan scowled at him. "I'll see you soon, Sonia."

"Thank you for visiting with me, Hunter. Have fun."

Hunter smiled at Sonia and then frowned at Juan before he walked back to the party.

"He's sweet on you," Juan said, none too happy.

"No, he'll find himself a young woman who is allowed in town." Her voice was filled with bitterness. She took a deep breath. "I'm glad you're here."

Juan sat down next to her and helped feed Brent. Brent wiped his greasy fingers on Juan's shirt and face. While Sonia was horrified, Juan laughed.

"This little one has made strides in just a day. Do you mind if I ask you why he didn't crawl or talk before?"

She was quiet for a moment. "I held him as much as I could. I didn't encourage him to talk. I was afraid Roger would slap him." Her hand shook as she tried to sip some water.

Juan took the cup and held it for her so she could drink. He tried to look calm while he was inwardly seething. "I hate to say it, but I'm glad Roger is dead. He sounds hateful."

She ducked her head. "Yes, he was," she whispered.

He put his finger under her chin and lifted her face so he could gaze into her eyes. "You're safe now."

She started to smile and it turned into a laugh as Brent took a handful of grapes and began to shove them into Juan's mouth. Brent laughed and laughed, and Juan couldn't help himself, he laughed too.

He noticed the looks they got from others at the party but he didn't care. He just hoped that she felt the same way. She appeared happy.

Brent crawled onto Juan's lap and held up his arms. Juan quickly lifted the boy up and hugged him. Brent laid his head oh Juan's shoulder. "Papa, love?"

Juan stroked the boy's back. He felt tears at the back of his eyes. "Yes, Papa loves you." Before long, Brent fell asleep.

"I'm so sorry, Juan. He's put you in an awful situation. I'll explain to him that he can't call you Papa. It's not right." Her face was so full of worry that he reached out and stroked her cheek.

"It's fine. I'll be gone most of next month. You can come and stay at my place while I'm away if you like."

"That's a long time to be away." She gave him a sidelong glance.

"I have horses to catch, and that takes time. Greg isn't able to go as much with Mercy and Hannah at home but he takes a turn here and there. I like being alone at times. If not for Carlos, I think I'd have left a long time ago. I like it here, but there are so many orphans."

"I'll ask Lynn about my staying at your place."

"Do you know how to shoot a gun and a rifle?"

She nodded. "My father took me hunting with him a few times. My mother soon put an end to it, saying it wasn't ladylike. But I went enough to learn."

"Out here, you need to know how to protect and feed yourself. You already know that. I bet by the time I come back, Brent will be walking."

There was a twinkle in her eye. "He just might at that."

Smitty joined them, and after a look between the two of them, he eased Brent into his arms. "Go dance you two."

Sonia appeared surprised and it seemed as though she was going to say no. Juan stood and put his hand out for her to take. She took a long look into his eyes before she nodded and took his hand. He didn't know what she was looking for but she must have found it.

"We won't be long," Sonia told Smitty.

"Two dances minimum. Don't worry about me. I've twirled my love around the dance floor all evening." He nodded toward the grassy area where folks were dancing. "It's your turn." His voice was filled with affection.

Juan gave her hand a quick squeeze as they walked toward the music and dancing. Suddenly she stopped.

"What if they stare at us or start talking about us?"

"It won't matter. I'll be dancing with the most beautiful woman here." The pleased expression on her face made him feel ten feet tall.

Her eyes widened as he started to dance.

He smiled. "You thought I didn't know how to dance didn't you?"

"Well, yes."

"Ma made sure we all knew the 'social graces,' as she calls them."

The feeling of her soft body in his arms scared him. He'd never felt this way before. He never thought to like a woman, but Sonia made it easy. She was beautiful and kind. He suddenly felt her stiffen and looked around them to see what had upset her. He watched as her parents danced close to them, gave them a dirty look, and then walked away from the rest of the dancers without looking back.

The raw pain on Sonia's face was hard to bear. He held her closer, but that just brought more attention their way. He tried to make it through the first dance, but he could feel her body jerk in silent sobs. He moved them to the edge of the dance area and then let go of her all except for her hand. He melted with her into the darkness and led her to a fallen log to sit on. He put his arms around her and it was as though a cloud burst inside of her. He felt his shirt grow wet but he didn't care.

He wasn't sure what to say to her. He could tell her that her parents didn't matter, but obviously they did. She cared what people thought of her, and it probably didn't help that she was with him. Maybe if she'd been dancing with Hunter, it wouldn't have been so bad. He was foolish to have thought he could be among the white people and nothing would be said.

He'd done her a disservice by being her friend. He touched her soft hair, knowing it would be the last time he'd touch her. She'd come to mean too much to him, and that couldn't be. He couldn't allow Brent to call him Papa anymore. He relished the feel of her in his arms but it had to end for her sake. People could be forgiving, and maybe even her indiscretion would eventually be forgiven, but they'd never forgive her if she married him.

Slowly he let her go and the agony in his heart grew. "We'd best get back. Brent will want you."

She tried to smile through her tears as she nodded. "Brent will be missing his papa too."

"I've given the whole thing some thought, and it isn't right for him to call me Papa."

"What?"

"I'm not the boy's father, and if I ever have kids of my own, what would they think?" He held his breath wishing he didn't have to lie to her.

She jerked away from him and stood. "Fine. I understand. Good night, Juan." She dashed the tears from her eyes with her fingers then turned and regally walked away.

He let out his breath and hung his head. It was better this way. They were getting too close, and people would never accept her again if they stayed together. Besides, he just wanted to be alone.

But somehow when she left, she took a piece of his heart with her. He'd never see Brent walk, hear him learn more words, never put him in the saddle for the first time. No, Juan would have to avoid her at all cost. He wouldn't be able to deny his love again if he saw her. How stupid could he have been, asking her to stay at his cabin while he was away?

With his heart in his throat, he saddled his horse and went home.

SONIA HURRIED to where Smitty sat and gently took her son. "Thank you."

His brow furrowed. "Where's Juan? Why didn't he walk you back here?"

"He doesn't want me, and he doesn't want Brent calling him Papa. He plans to have a family of his own one day, and he made it clear his plans do not include me or Brent." She shook her head. "I don't know what happened. My parents snubbed us on the dance floor, and I ended up in Juan's arms crying. Now he's gone, and now any of the foolish dreams I spun around him are gone too. Good night, Smitty."

She skirted the edges of the party on the way to the house and went to her room. The cradle had been brought up, and she was relieved. She got Brent ready for bed, and put him in his cradle. Then she took off the pretty dress she'd worn and put on her nightgown. She grabbed a handkerchief she'd put with Brent's things and got into bed.

The laughter and music drifted through the window, happy sounds of celebration, and that made her all the sadder. Why would Juan act as though he had some claim on her in front of his brothers and then tell her he had plans that didn't include her? She'd suffered a lot of pain the last few years, but this by far hurt the most. She'd gotten her hopes up, and now she was once again thrown away.

Was there something unlikeable about her? Certainly someone would have told her by now if she was mean. She was friendless, and the thought tightened her chest. She had never been a social butterfly but to have no one…it hurt. The Settlers were kind to her, but they weren't close the way friends were. The way she thought she had been with Juan.

Had she mistaken the happiness and love she saw in his eyes? She'd probably only seen what she wanted to see and she had been mistaken. Tears kept flowing, and soon enough her handkerchief was soaked. She took a deep breath and tried to sleep.

CHAPTER FOUR

Juan pulled his bandana over his mouth and nose and drew his hat down in front as the wind blew harder, engulfing him in swirls of dust. He kept careful hold on his string of horses as he rode Journey toward a grouping of boulders. They'd have to shelter there to wait the dust storm out, and he wasn't in the mood to stand still.

The last horse in the string was a big bay, and he wanted nothing to do with the dust or the rocks. It took some doing, but Juan finally pulled him to safety. His original plan was to leave a week later, but he'd left the day after the party. He couldn't sort out his feelings and balance them against what was best for Sonia. Time apart should help.

Greg was back home building a second corral. After he finished that, he would start breaking the horses they already had. It was a lot of work, but so was catching the horses. Juan grabbed his canteen and slid down to the base of the rocks. He drank the much-needed water and thought of Sonia.

If he was being truthful with himself, he'd been a coward in the way he handled Sonia last night. She probably thought him to be downright hateful. Well, he had been hateful, and he'd gotten what he wanted hadn't he? His heart squeezed. Sure he had. She probably never wanted to see him again.

If things were different, he'd grab her up and kiss her like there was no tomorrow, but things weren't different. Society wouldn't accept a relationship between them. He'd be better off without a wife and family. He had a family with the Settlers. And he was lucky to have them. Hopefully, he hadn't put them in an awkward situation with Sonia and Brent.

Journey nickered, and the hair on the back of Juan's neck stood up. Someone was out there. He stood and using his hand to shield his eyes a bit, he recognized Carlos. He waved his arms in the air trying to catch his attention. It was a relief to see Carlos nod at him.

As soon as Carlos was close enough, Juan dragged him out of his saddle. "What in tarnation do you think you're doing? You could have gotten lost out here. Where are your supplies? I should smack you upside the head, but I won't."

"I had to come. I couldn't stay at the big house. Your girlfriend cried all night. I know because her bed is just on the other side of the wall from mine. She tried to be quiet, but I heard her. I didn't want to be there when questions were asked. I left Pa a note." Carlos flashed him a smile. "I know you're glad to see me."

Juan sat back down. She'd cried all night? That was his fault.

Carlos joined him on the ground. "So what happened? Did you try to steal a kiss?"

Juan almost chuckled. "If I stole a kiss, she'd be smiling. I told her I didn't want Brent calling me Papa."

Carlos' eyes grew wide. "Whatcha go and do that for?"

"I wanted her to stop liking me. There isn't a future for us. She's had a hard enough time. It wouldn't be right for her to get involved with a Mexican."

JUAN

Carlos' shoulders slumped. "I know. I'll never have a wife either. What were our folks thinking being on a wagon train full of white people? If it were me, I'd have traveled south toward Mexico. There are bound to be people like us down there."

"You're right about that. I think Pa just wanted a place of his own. He and Ma worked for the Stewarts for years and they wanted to be owners instead of servants. I don't blame them wanting a fresh start. They must have saved every penny they ever made to afford the trip to Oregon. It should have been a fresh start. But, if you remember, no one ever helped them. When they both got sick, no one would come to doctor them. I often wonder if they could have been saved." A somber feeling clouded over him.

"At least Lynn and Smitty took us into their wagon, even if it was already filled with orphans. It's funny, those kids never looked at us as different. I do remember a few on the wagon train telling Ma she couldn't take us in, but she refused to give in. If Sonia doesn't think of you as different, why not let her be your sweetheart?"

"Did you see how people treated us and looked at us last night? Even her parents gave us dirty looks and then walked off, as though they couldn't be dancing if we were. I don't want that for her or for Brent."

"Did it ever occur to you that maybe it was her they were reacting to? You have to admit she's had a mixed up life."

Juan didn't want to talk about it anymore. "The storm's passed, and we have a ways to go before we see any horses. Good thing I packed a lot of supplies."

"I figured you did."

"What if you couldn't find me?"

Carlos shrugged. "I would have turned around and gone home."

Juan shook his head. "Mount up." What was it like to not

have a care in the world? It seemed as though he'd always had others to consider before he made decisions.

They rode for hours until it was almost dark. When they stopped, Juan quickly got a fire going and taught Carlos how to make coffee. They fried up some of the ham Juan had brought. Juan also tried his hand at making biscuits. They were a bit tough to get their teeth through, but if they dipped them in coffee they were edible.

"I thought for sure we'd be eating beans the whole time," Carlos commented after they cleaned everything up.

"I brought the ham and some bacon. As soon as those are gone we'll move on to cans of beans."

Carlos flashed him another grin. "I don't suppose you have an extra bedroll."

"No, I don't, but I do have an extra blanket you can use." Juan grabbed it from the pile of supplies and threw it at Carlos.

"I don't think we need to stand guard tonight, but as we get farther out we will."

Carlos furrowed his brow. "What were you planning to do if I wasn't here? Not sleep?"

"I wouldn't have made such a big fire advertising where I was camping." Juan laid out his bedroll and lay down. He closed his eyes and listened to Carlos settle in for the night. Then all he heard was the chirping of crickets and distant howls of wolves. Some big game passed by close to them, but kept going. He relived having Sonia in his arms again as they'd danced. She had curves in all the right places, and her hair smelled heavenly. It had been so perfect. He turned onto his side. Perfect until he'd ruined it. Even though it was for their own good, it smarted. She'd cried all night, and the guilt over that hit him hard.

He squeezed his eyes tight, willing himself to clear his mind and fall asleep. He had horses to catch and he'd best keep his mind on that. And now that Carlos was there, he had him to look after and teach. Tomorrow they'd head to the canyon he'd used to keep the horses as he caught them. Hopefully the gate he'd made would still be there.

Sonia rocked Brent on the front porch. Smitty had just found Carlos' note and wasn't too happy about the way Carlos had gone about leaving. If he'd asked, Smitty said, it would have been fine. All Sonia could think of was the fact that Juan had run as quickly from her as he could. Her heart was in tatters, but for Brent's sake she smiled.

She'd been on the receiving end of curious glances the whole day. No doubt they'd heard her crying all night. She was embarrassed that she'd become a burden to them all. One thing she knew. She wouldn't be staying at Juan's house while he was gone.

She picked up her cup of coffee and drank a bit. The sun was going down, and the beautiful display of orange, yellow and purple soothed her soul a bit. God sure knew what he was doing when he made sunrise and sunset. It was a time she often reflected and prayed.

The door opened and then shut quietly, and Sonia knew without looking it was Lynn. Lynn had a cup of coffee in her hand too. She sat in one of the rocking chairs closest to Sonia and was silent for a while.

It would have been nice, but Sonia's stomach clenched, wondering what Lynn would have to say about her and Brent.

"Juan and Carlos will probably be gone for about a week. I'm surprised Juan didn't shoo Carlos back home. Juan likes his alone time." She sipped her coffee and rocked for a few moments. "It sounds like you wanted more than Juan was willing to give."

So here it was. "I misread him, I guess. I've caught him staring at me, and he was so kind." Sonia took a deep breath to keep from crying. "When we danced together he held me close, and I was too fanciful. I thought it meant something. But he let me know in no uncertain terms that he didn't want anything to do with me or Brent." She lifted one shoulder in a half-shrug. "I suppose he realized I was a bad person when he saw how others treated me. I don't blame him, it just hurts so much."

"I'm sorry it happened. He let Brent call him Papa. I thought he was thinking about marrying you." Lynn reached out and patted Sonia's arm.

Sonia shook her head and frowned. "He told me he didn't want Brent to call him Papa anymore." Her chin quivered.

Lynn's sigh was heavy. "I don't think you misread him. But he has a hard time getting close to people. He thinks no one could possibly love him. He allows my hugs, but he shies away from others. From the time we met, he's been a loner except for his brother, Carlos. I think perhaps he had the best intentions, but couldn't follow through and for that I'm sorry." Lynn gave her a sad smile.

"It was the way I was treated by the guests at the party. I'd been through it so many times. People say hurtful things, and if Juan had any idea that I was a good woman, he learned otherwise." She drew a shaky breath. "Even my parents made a show of hatred. I'm not sure what to do now. I can't accept your charity anymore. I do appreciate all you've done for me and Brent. I need to earn some money and make a fresh start."

"Don't rush and make a bad decision. We enjoy having you here." Lynn's voice was warm and sweet.

"Thank you." It would be so tempting to stay indefinitely.

JUAN

"But I just don't want to be the reason Juan doesn't come to see you. I'll figure something out. I'd best get my little one to bed. Thank you for your kindness, Lynn."

"Good night."

Sonia nodded as she stood with a sleeping Brent in her arms and went into the house. The cradles were all upstairs so she climbed the steps. Hunter hurried over and took Brent from her.

"He's getting heavy."

"He certainly is. Thank you for your help." She didn't like the starry-eyed look he gave her. It wouldn't do for Hunter to get mixed up with her. She watched him put Brent into the cradle. "Good night." She quickly went to the door and held it open. Thankfully, Hunter left right away.

She put on her nightgown, considered Hunter's possible growing feelings, and came to the realization she needed to leave within the next day or two. She didn't want to be the cause of any other problems.

JUAN ALMOST LAUGHED AT CARLOS' impatience. Tracking horses and gaining their trust was a long process. The herd he was tracking had a strong black stallion followed by almost twenty mares. The stallion would be a problem if he brought him home. Greg would try to break him, and that stallion was mean.

It took Juan much longer than usual to become part of the herd. He'd had to leave Journey with Carlos at the canyon and ride one of the mares he brought. It took four days to get the ornery stallion to accept him. Today was the day, and he hoped Carlos would ready with the gate open when he drove the horses toward the canyon.

He tried to rope the lead mare, the stallion's favorite, and the whole herd started to run in the direction of the canyon. He rode low and chased the horses until they were starting to tire. He hoped his mare had enough stamina. She usually did well.

As he got closer to the canyon, he saw Carlos open the gate and as they rode through he slowed his mare, jumped down and helped Carlos close and secure the gate.

"I've never seen the likes before," Carlos said, his voice full of excitement. His eyes twinkled as he smiled.

"It's like riding faster than the wind. Nothing comes close to the feeling of running with the horses." Juan watched the stallion. He'd notice soon enough he was trapped. There was a small pool of water at the very back of the canyon. "Could you take care of the mare while I watch the stallion?"

Carlos nodded. "Why do you have to watch him?"

"As soon as he comes to the conclusion he's fenced in, he'll make some attempt to escape. I'll discourage him with the whip."

"You'd whip a horse?"

"No I whip the gate and it keeps the horses back. The first time I made the gate too low and the stallion easily jumped it and bit my shoulder. He then whistled for the rest of his herd to follow. So not only was I bleeding badly, I had nothing to show for it."

Carlos' eyes widened. "How come you never told me?"

Juan shrugged. "I didn't want you worrying every time I left to gather more horses."

The stallion stared at the gate and charged toward it, veering off before he slammed into it. He then walked alongside the gate, examining it for an exit. He whistled angrily and reared up three times. Finally he came back to the gate and pushed on it with its barrel chest. It moved but not enough.

Juan got out the whip and began hitting the wooden

structure. He walked up and down a few times using the whip. The horses stayed back.

"Wow, those horses sure don't like that," Carlos said.

"I'll have to use the sorrel I brought to cut the horses I want from the herd and get going."

"So soon? The horses are tired," Carlos protested.

"It's the best time. We won't go fast but we need to put some distance between us and that stallion." Keeping a careful eye on the stallion, Juan cut ten horses from the herd. He put them on two strings, one for Carlos to handle and the other one for him. He then saddled Journey and waited for Carlos to mount his own horse.

"You're not going to leave the horses in the canyon are you?"

Juan shook his head. "I have a much smaller canyon I use not too far from here. I usually drive the horses I cut into it and let them rest for the day. I come back to this canyon right away and let the other horses go."

They rode for a little over an hour and secured the horses in the smaller canyon. Juan then rode back and released the other horses. The stallion made a move to come after him but Juan swung the whip and hit the ground a few times and finally the stallion drove the herd away in the direction they had originally come from.

Juan admired the stallion. He was well muscled and big. He'd make fine horses when bred, but it wasn't worth Greg getting hurt again. Mercy would horsewhip him if he brought such a powerful animal back with him. He turned Journey and went to join Carlos.

He smiled when he saw that Carlos had set up camp and was heating up the beans. Having a partner sure was easier than going it alone. For a moment, he thought of Sonia. She would have made a good partner but it wasn't meant to be. It would be hard to see her on the ranch, but at least she'd be safe.

THE MOON WAS full and it lit her way. Sonia had been very careful to be quiet when she left the Settlers' house. She did the same thing Carlos had done. She left a note. It was a lie about how she'd found a job and would be fine. She thanked them too. The only place she had to go was the shack she had lived in with her husband. She hoped and prayed that her father-in-law wasn't still there.

If she stayed at the shack, no one would look for her. No one would be able to mention seeing her. She jostled Brent to the other shoulder. He was getting heavy. It was the bounty of food the Settlers had shared with them.

She decided to stay on the road even though it was longer. Going through the woods would be too nerve racking. She doubted she'd meet anyone on her way. The only thing she had was the blanket Juan had given her for Brent. She'd left the clothes they let her borrow behind and left wearing the tattered gray dress she had arrived in. She'd had time to mend it, but it still looked like a rag.

She walked for a long time before she stopped. She didn't remember the walk to be so far. Finding a big flat rock near the side of the road, she sat on it. But sitting led to thinking. It wasn't a good idea to go to the shack, she knew that. But it was the only idea open to her. The Settlers needed their son in their lives, and he wouldn't come around if she was there. It was that simple.

Her arms ached as she stood back up and continued walking. She'd taken a hunting knife from Smitty before she left. She'd have to replace it as soon as she could. But for now, it would give her some protection in case Wendell was still living in the shack.

Noises came from the woods as if she was being tracked by an animal. Feeling uneasy, she walked faster. Once again, she shifted Brent to the other shoulder. It couldn't be much farther. Grateful for the moonlight, she kept going. By the time the shack came into sight she was beyond exhausted.

The shack was completely dark. Hopefully, the lack of light was a good sign. Fear filled her as she reluctantly stood at the door. Fatigue crowded out the little voice in the back of her mind telling her to turn and run.

Slowly, she opened the wooden door and then quickly looked around. It smelled like rotting food, but there was no sign of Wendell. She let out the breath she hadn't realized she'd been holding in. A rat scurried across the floor and luckily raced out the front door, which she promptly shut. She laid Brent down on the bed, found the lamp and lit it. Next, she laid a fire in the fireplace. There wasn't a cook stove. She had always cooked over the fire. She lit the fire and grabbed an empty pail. Giving Brent a long look she then hurried out the door to the water pump.

They'd have somewhere to lay their heads that night, and she was grateful. After going back into the house, she immediately locked the door. She poured the water into an iron pot and placed it on a hook that was attached to the crane and swung the arm of the crane over the fire. She'd have warm water soon.

In the light she could see just how filthy the cabin was, but it wasn't anything lye soap and hard work wouldn't fix. For the first time, she was glad the shack was tucked away in the trees and away from other homes.

Before, when Roger had hit her, she'd wished that someone was close enough to hear her cries. But now she was hoping that it would take a while before anyone even knew she was there. She'd set some traps tomorrow and hopefully she'd catch a rabbit for dinner. She had planted a garden before Roger died and hopefully some of the vegetables were still there.

She looked in a small tin box she'd stashed behind the other items on the shelf. It was actually a crate nailed to the wall but it was functional. She smiled when she opened the box. Her precious tea was still in it. She made herself some tea and then poured some of the water in a chipped basin. The soap was still there. Wendell obviously didn't like to be clean.

A clean towel was on one of the other shelves and she used it to wash her face. She unbuttoned the top of her dress and quickly washed up. She'd sleep in her clothes. Someone might see the smoke coming from the chimney and try to come in. By right it was her cabin and land, small as it was. Roger never claimed the maximum acreage he was entitled to under the Oregon land grant. He had no ambition to better himself.

It was just as well now. She had no livestock to care for, though a couple of chickens would have been nice. It was something she could work toward. In the next few days, she'd trap for raccoons. The coonskin hat was still popular, and she could trade them for food. Not in town of course but there was a trading post about six miles away toward the north. Meanwhile, she'd make due.

She sat in an uncomfortable chair in front of the fire and fell asleep.

When morning came around, she washed the floors first so Brent could crawl around. She also put the chairs in front of the fire blocking it from Brent's explorations. Next, she scrubbed every surface in the cabin. She took the two tick mattresses and put them outside to air. She would need to wash them down with the strong soap too.

Next, she made a big fire outside and set the laundry tub on top of it. After hauling water, she set Brent on his blanket under a tree. He fell asleep instantly. Grabbing all the bed linens and anything else that had been used in the shack, she dumped it all into the hot water. After adding the soap, she stirred the laundry around with a big paddle then allowed the water to boil. She wanted all vermin dead and removed from the sheets.

It took a good portion of the day, but she got it done, and soon the wash was hanging on a fraying rope drying in the breeze. They only thing waiting was the garden and to check the traps. Brent looked like he was in a deep sleep, so she slipped away to the nearby traps. The first three yielded nothing but she got lucky on the last one.

She was able to skin the rabbit before Brent woke. She'd cure the skin, it might be made into something she could trade.

Brent woke and yelled "Mama." He smiled in delight when he saw her. Her heart filled as she picked him up and kissed him.

"You slept a long time."

"Long," he repeated.

"Would you like to play in the garden with me?"

He shrugged his shoulders.

"How about play in the dirt?" she asked.

"Me play!"

She'd checked the garden earlier and except for a major weed problem there were still a lot of vegetables left. Anything that had grown above ground had been eaten by animals, probably rats, but there were turnips, potatoes and onions to dig up. There were also carrots, parsnips, rutabagas, yams, and beets.

They'd be just fine. She'd been gone long enough for the vegetables to grow. Some people had never heard of beets and rutabagas but Sonia had come across the seeds while working in her parents' store and had put some away for herself. Luckily, she remembered to take them when they disowned her.

Roger hadn't been impressed. Too bad for him. She pulled up an onion as well as a few carrots and potatoes. It was enough for one day. She might not have money, but she was wealthy in vegetables. Maybe she could sell some if needed.

She watched Brent dig the soil with an old spoon she'd given him. He was a happy child.

"Come on, we need to get inside."

He shook his head. "No!"

She laughed. "What do you mean no. Be a good boy for Mama."

He stared at her and put dirt in his mouth. He tried to spit it out but ended up crying instead. "Papa. Me want Papa."

She picked him up and brought him inside. After cleaning out his mouth, her tears wanted to fall. Sonia dashed away the first few and got a hold of herself. How could she explain why Brent had a papa one day and didn't have one the next?

She gave him a bowl and a wooden spoon to play with, and he forgot his question. Hopefully, she'd never cross paths with Juan again, and Brent could forget him.

CHAPTER FIVE

"Open the gate!" Juan called to Greg. The sound of the horses' hooves was loud, and the dust they kicked up was enough to choke a man. But Juan and Carlos had driven the horses home. They'd made it.

Greg opened the gate to the corral wide and stood aside as the horses ran into the fenced-in area. He quickly closed the gate when the last horse entered.

Juan jumped down off Journey and strode to the fence where Greg stood. "We got some good mares. In a few years we'll be rich!"

"Those are some of the finest I've seen." Greg took off his hat and wiped his brow. "How did Carlos do?"

Juan smiled, feeling like a proud father. "It's in his blood. He was a natural. How'd Ma and Pa take it that he left?"

"They were concerned. If he'd left with you it wouldn't have been a problem. Ma was sure he'd get lost and never find you. Pa was much calmer but they'll be relieved to see him home again."

Juan and Greg stared at the magnificent creatures milling about the corral.

"Greg, it was the best!" Carlos enthused as he joined them. "Juan is magic with those wild horses. He taught me a lot. I'm going to see if I can live here with him!"

Greg's brow rose in surprise as Juan shrugged his shoulders. "Maybe one day, Carlos, but I doubt Ma will want to let you go," Juan said. He nodded his head toward the two riders headed his way. It would have been a dream come true if Sonia was one of them.

As they got closer he saw it was his parents. "Hope you're not in too much trouble, Carlos," he teased.

Carlos' eyes widened as he grimaced. "I knew I'd be in big trouble, but I had to go. I just had to."

They watched as their pa swung down off his horse and then helped their ma down. Carlos took a step behind Juan.

"Nice horses. You do have an eye for them, Juan," Pa said.

Ma walked up and glared at both him and Carlos. She shook her head and then she ran toward Carlos and hugged him.

Juan smiled while Carlos was getting the stuffing hugged out of him.

"I was so worried, Carlos." Ma said as she released him.

Pa stepped forward and put his arm around his wife's waist. "Son, sneaking out and leaving a note is not the right way to do things."

Carlos hung his head. "I really wanted to go."

"The thing is, you caused needless worry. We always talk things out. I would have allowed you to go if Juan approved," Pa explained. He let go of his wife and hugged Carlos to him. "I'm just glad you're all right." He scanned the young boy up and down before he nodded.

"If that's the way then I want to live with Juan." He jutted his chin out.

Before his parents could say anything, Juan started to

talk. "I told Carlos maybe someday. I know he has school to finish."

Carlos narrowed his eyes at Juan and finally shook his head.

"How're Sonia and Brent?" Juan asked, unable to contain his worry.

Ma bit her lip before she spoke. "She left us a note too. We don't know where she went. Your pa has searched, but there's no sign of them. We really don't know why she left. I thought I'd reassured her that she was more than welcome to stay. I've been worried about them too. Juan, I thought the two of you were getting close."

Guilt choked Juan. He stared at the ground, unable to meet his ma's gaze. "I told her there was no future for us, and I didn't say it as nicely as I should."

"You didn't like her?" his pa asked. "You could have fooled me. I saw the way you two looked at each other."

Juan brought his head up. "I'm not looking for a wife."

His parents exchanged glances then walked to their horses. His pa helped Ma into the saddle. "Carlos, we expect you home tonight," he said firmly and then swung himself onto his horse.

"Yes, sir," Carlos responded glumly.

They watched them ride away in silence.

"Well, are we going to work the horses?" Carlos asked with hope in his eyes.

"No, not today," Greg said, shaking his head. "We let them rest for a few days."

"I might as well get going then." Carlos kicked the dirt and mounted his horse without glancing at either of them.

"He'll get over it," Greg said.

"I know. I'm going to clean up."

"Go ahead. I'll take care of Journey and the pack horses."

Juan nodded. "Thanks."

He walked to his house. Maybe Sonia was hiding there again. When he opened the door he was greeted by silence. He quickly looked around and there was no sign of them. Worried, he sank onto a chair, put his elbows on his knees, and cradled his head in his hands. He hadn't thought she'd leave. She had nowhere to go. What was she thinking taking Brent to heaven knew where?

His heart squeezed. It was all his fault. He shouldn't have been so mean to her. Where could she be? All he wanted to do was to protect her. People already snubbed her and it would have been worse if she was with him. How would Brent feel when he grew up and no one would play with him?

The house was silent, almost too silent. He'd craved the quiet and being alone. But now all he felt was lonely. Shaking his head, he stood up and grabbed his hat. He squashed it down on his head and went out the door. She had to be somewhere, and he was going to find her. What was she thinking going off to who knew where with Brent? She could be hurt or scared or maybe she was hungry. He needed to find her.

SONIA STIFFENED as the door swung open. Fear clutched at her when she saw Wendell entering the shack. She'd had hoped that he was gone for good. From the anger in his eyes, she knew she was in trouble. She glanced over at Brent and was relieved to see that he was still sleeping.

"What do you think you're doing in my house?" demanded Wendell. His boots kicked up dirt as he walked toward her.

He smelled of days of unwashed sweat. He hadn't shaved, and his eyes were bloodshot. He must've been on some type of bender. She almost gagged as his putrid scent overwhelmed her. She needed to stand her ground and act unafraid, though that was easier said than done.

He tried to grab her but she took a step back, and the fury on his face gave her pause. Antagonizing Wendell would do no good. He glared at her. She'd be lucky to get out of the cabin in one piece.

Her stomach dropped. She had just started to let her guard down, and now he was here. She glanced at the distance from where she stood to Brent to the door. The odds weren't in her favor.

"I figured you had abandoned the cabin. After all you haven't been here in over a week. I thought Brent and I could make a life for ourselves here. But we can just go. I don't want to get in your way." Sonia slowly walked over to the bed. Before she could reach Brent, Wendell grabbed her shoulder and squeezed it. Pain instantly shot through her as he pulled her back against him.

"You're not going anywhere. I knew all along you'd be back, and I've been waiting. There ain't nobody out there for you. You're considered trash now, and there's no redeeming yourself." His humorless laugh sent chills along her back. "So it looks like you're mine, and I can do whatever I want. Nobody cares and nobody is gonna save you. So you can just get your ideas of leaving out of your head." He spun her around until they were face-to-face and he stared at her with his beady eyes. A nasty leer twisted his features.

Sonia didn't know what to do. She needed to protect Brent at all costs. And the cost was going to be high, too high but she'd do what she had to. "I'm sure we can all live here peacefully. I can cook and clean and earn my keep. I don't see any reason for violence." She tried to take a step back, but he grabbed her arm and searing pain shot into her shoulder.

She cried out.

"Violence? We can avoid violence if you do everything I say. We'll just act as if we were married. You do know what it means to be married, don't you? You must obey your husband in all things. And if you don't, your boy'll pay the price. He'll learn what discipline is, if I don't decide to up and kill him," Wendell chuckled.

Sonia's body stiffened. The viselike grip he had on her arm would leave bruises, and it was just the beginning. Last time she had been lucky. He passed out after beating her. She'd taken Brent and snuck away, but he likely wouldn't pass out a second time. She didn't know what to do. Biding her time might be the best course of action. She couldn't risk her son getting hurt or killed. Why, oh, why had she left the Settler's house? Her broken heart would have mended eventually. But Wendell was capable of leaving lasting scars.

"I made some rabbit stew if you'd like some," she offered trying to smile.

Wendell studied her, probably trying to figure out if she was going to obey him or not.

"Why don't I pour some hot water in a basin so you can clean up? You left some clothes here that I washed." She couldn't stand the smell of him anymore. "If you let go of my arm I can grab the soap and a towel for you." She stood as still as she could. He held on for a minute more before he let her go. She longed to rub her arm but she forced herself to resist. She didn't want to give Wendell any more satisfaction that he'd hurt her.

Wendell smiled, showing off his brown teeth. "Maybe you'd like to help me get cleaned up and changed." He winked at her and gave her chills.

She took a deep breath. It was all for Brent. As long as he

didn't get hurt she could stand anything. She went to the fireplace and poured water that had been heating, into a basin. Next, she put the basin on the table and grabbed a towel and some soap. Thankfully, there were two bars and she wouldn't have to use the same one Wendell used. She put these on the table as well.

"Why don't you get started while I get your clothes for you?"

"You do that, honey, and then you can help me. I've been a itchin' and a scratchin' for days now. As soon as I'm clean, we can have a bit of fun together." He smiled obviously enjoying tormenting her.

He took off his shirt and started to wash himself. Sonia had never seen so much hair on a man in her whole life. He looked more like a grizzly than a man. No wonder he was desperate to have her, no other woman would want him.

After putting his clothes on the table she took a step back. Her body shook at the thought of helping him. Brent turned over in his sleep and her resolve to do whatever was necessary hardened. Wendell was a nasty piece of business but she planned on walking out of the cabin one day.

"I can't say that I really miss Roger all that much. How about you?" Wendell asked.

"Of course I miss him he was my husband." She hoped that God would forgive her lies.

"Oh, really? He beat on you plenty. Maybe even more than me. I used to have to teach his mama many a lesson. Nothing I ever did was right, so I got her to shut up. It wasn't any of her business where I went at night. The people in the saloon were always glad to see me but she thought I should stay home. I cured her of that notion pretty fast. In fact, I cured her of most notions that she had. She walked around with black eyes most of the time but it was her own fault. A man must take charge." He lathered up his hairy chest and arms before he rinsed the soap off. He threw the cloth at her. "You can do my back."

Sonia swallowed hard. Everything within her said no, but she had to ignore the warnings. She rinsed out the cloth and lathered soap onto it. Then she washed his back. She was glad that she was behind him so he couldn't see her cringing. Somehow or other she'd escape but she needed a plan.

"That feels good, girl. Perhaps it's time for you to wash the rest of me."

"I've been thinking about you, and I think we got off to the wrong start. We should probably get to know each other first before I see any more of you. You know, how real couples do it. I think we could have a good life together."

Wendell stared at her and then he shrugged his shoulders. "I'll think about it. Now you go sit on the bed with your son. You can watch or not, I really don't care."

Sonia practically ran to the bed and sat with her back facing toward Wendell. She tried to take slow even breaths but she couldn't relax with Wendell in the house. She gazed at her son and smiled. He was her treasure and she'd figure something out. It was going to have to be soon, though.

Juan didn't know where Sonia was. It was like she'd disappeared. She was nowhere he'd looked, and no one had admitted to seeing her or hearing about her. Remembering her mentioning it once, he had gone to the saloon and was relieved to discover that she didn't work there. He'd even gone so far as to check with her parents. When he'd gone into the store they had sniffed the air as if he smelled bad. But he was used to that behavior from them. They really didn't give him an answer; they just glared at him. But he suspected from their surprised expressions they had no idea either.

Where could she have gone?

He led Journey down the town's main street. And then, outside the barbershop, he heard it: Wendell Plank's name. It sounded as though he owed people money and he'd made a lot of people mad. When they started talking about lynching Wendell, Juan hightailed it out of there before there was any thought of lynching *him*. But now he knew where he needed to go. He only hoped he wasn't too late.

He mounted Journey and took off at a gallop toward the shack that Sonia used to live in. If that coward laid one finger on her, he was gonna kill him. How stupid! He should have checked there first. He just hadn't thought she would ever go back there.

She'd been gone for about a week, so he wasn't sure what type of condition she'd be in. And what about Brent? Fear for them both tightened all of his muscles, and Juan spurred his horse on.

It seemed to take forever to get to the shack. It was starting to get dark, and he could see the fire in the fireplace between the slats of the house. How did they live there during the winter? She must've froze. He jumped down from his horse and tied him a little ways from the house. Then, as silently as he could, he rounded to the side of the shack. He looked between the slats and saw Wendell, Sonia, and Brent sitting at the table eating. Sonia's face didn't seem to have any bruises on it. Relief spread through Juan's body. At least she wasn't hurt.

He didn't know much about Wendell. He probably had a gun in there, and he'd be the type to shoot first and ask questions later. He figured him for a coward since he hit women. Maybe he should just knock on the door, but would that get him shot? Or cause trouble for her? Hearing an owl hoot nearby, he shook his head. That was his girl in there with her son, and he aimed to get her out of there.

His breathing hitched. His girl? If he had claimed her in the first place she wouldn't be in there with Wendell. This was his fault. He shouldn't have turned her away from him. He peered through the crack again. She seemed subdued. And Brent was sitting close to her as if he was afraid to get to close to Wendell.

No, Juan had to be careful here. He decided to keep watch on them. If Wendell got out of hand he'd rush the door.

He waited, watching through the slats for a few minutes. She definitely wasn't the same girl who had started coming out of her shell when she and Brent were with his ma and pa. He was a fool for waiting. What if he waited and she got hurt? He wasn't going to knock on the door. Instead, he would go through with his gun drawn. If he was making a mistake, Sonia could tell him. But he doubted he was making a mistake.

As quietly as he could, Juan walked to the front of the cabin and drew his gun. He slowly opened the door and then rushed inside. And he caught Wendell with his pants down. He almost laughed.

"I've come to take the girl and her son off your hands." He kept his face impassive while he stared at Wendell.

Wendell quickly pulled on his pants and then his shirt. He sputtered and shook his head. "No one is taking my family from me 'specially not some Mexican."

Juan clenched his teeth and tightened his hold on his gun. It wouldn't do if Wendell thought he'd found a weakness. He pretended he didn't hear Wendell's slurs. Quickly, he gazed at Sonia. He wanted to be able to give her some signal that everything would be fine, but he didn't dare. Wendell was a bully, and if he thought Juan really wanted Sonia and Brent he'd keep them out of spite.

"I was looking for some help around my place, and I thought the girl would be perfect. I'd heard she'd fallen on hard times."

Wendell narrowed his eyes as he studied Juan. He tilted his head as though he was thinking of what he could get out of the deal. "Hey, aren't you the fella that has all those horses?"

Juan shrugged. "I have a few horses if that's what you mean. Most of them are already promised to the Army."

"Well, I can't just let you have her and the boy. They're definitely worth a horse or perhaps two. I mean who's gonna do my cooking and cleaning? A man's gotta have some comforts, you know." Wendell smiled as he scratched his belly.

Juan made a show of examining Sonia and Brent carefully. "I don't know, I think they're only worth one horse." Juan suppressed a smile when Sonia's jaw dropped.

Wendell stroked his chin then shook his head. "They're worth two, perhaps three even."

"Don't I get a say in any of this?" Sonia's voice was shaking.

Both men said, "No" at the same time.

The tears in her eyes brought a few curse words to Juan's mind, but he held his tongue. He wanted to spare her any more pain. He put his boot on a chair and leaned on his knee then cocked his right brow and stared at Wendell. "I can give you two, but they'd be unbroken. Or—no, never mind."

Wendell's eyes grew wide. "What do ya mean never mind? I want to know what else you was goin' to offer or no deal." He smiled; seeming certain he had the advantage.

Juan shrugged. "I do have one horse I might be able to give you. It's my horse, actually, and he's well trained. But I'm not sure. It isn't really a fair deal, my horse is worth far more than the girl and her son."

"Done! We've got ourselves a deal. Sonia, get your things. You and the brat are going with this Mexican." Wendell smiled and looked like he was about to do a jig. "Hurry now, we don't want to keep the man waiting. Sonia, hurry up. If you mess this up for me, you'll be sorry."

"I'm taking my saddle and my saddlebags with me. The horse's name is Journey, and I expect you to treat him right."

"Don't you think you can come here and tell me what to do. We have a deal, and the horse is mine. What I do with a horse is none of your business. Sonia, get out here before I get mad."

Sonia quickly filled a canvas bag with their meager belongings and then she picked up Brent. She looked from one man to the other before she raced out of the shack.

"I'll just come outside and make sure you keep our bargain. I wouldn't want you to steal your horse back." Wendell gave him a sickening smile.

Juan couldn't wait to get as far away from Wendell and his falling-down house as he could. He went out the door and without looking at Sonia or Brent he unsaddled Journey. He put the saddle up on his shoulder and held the saddlebag. Then he gave Wendell a curt nod and began to walk in the direction of his property.

He closed his eyes in relief when he heard Sonia and Brent scurrying behind him. He didn't dare acknowledge them. He just kept walking until Wendell and the shack were out of sight. He took a deep breath and put his saddlebag and saddle down on the ground. He turned, unsurprised at the look of doubt and fear he saw in Sonia's eyes.

"Sonia…" he murmured and held his arms open. To his relief she walked to him. After giving Sonia and Brent a quick hug, he kissed Sonia on the forehead. Then he dug into his saddlebag grabbed a clean bandanna and handed it to her.

"Thank you." Sonia wiped her tears with the bandanna. "I

can't allow you to trade Journey away. Your horse means so much to you, and you spent so much time training him. I'm going to return to Wendell so you can have your horse back." Her voice was so sad, and she looked as though she was about to sob.

"Papa!" Brent smiled happily as he waved his hands around.

"Brent, don't call him—"

"Come here Brent, let Papa hold you." Juan took Brent into his arms and kissed his cheek. "I've missed you. Would you like to come to my house?"

Brent crowed and nodded happily. He wrapped his little arms around Juan's neck and buried his face in his shoulder.

Sonia stared at the two of them. "I don't understand."

Juan smiled at her. "I couldn't leave you with Wendell. We both know he would beat you, and I suspect worse. This is the right solution for now, and we'll talk about it later. I want to get you home and rested. I want you to feel safe. I bet it's been a long week for you."

Sonia nodded and without a word picked up the saddlebag to carry.

Juan bent his knees and grabbed his saddle so he had Brent on one shoulder and the saddle on the other. He started walking, feeling good about what he'd just done. He wouldn't have to worry about Sonia for a while at least. The more he walked, the more he realized it wasn't relief he felt, it went deeper than that. He would have beaten Wendell if necessary. He chuckled.

Sonia gave him an inquisitive look. "What's so funny?"

"Wendell thinks he got the best part of the bargain."

CHAPTER SIX

The closer they got to Juan's house the more nervous Sonia became. She slowed her steps a bit trying to figure out a plan. They wouldn't be allowed to stay at Juan's house. What would people say? She frowned. They'd have a lot to say and none of it good.

Juan turned his whole body around and gave her an encouraging smile. "Come on, slowpoke, we're almost there." He didn't wait for an answer; he turned and kept walking.

Why was it no one cared if she was living in the same house with Wendell, but if she lived with Juan it would be scandalous? Wendell was a brute, and Juan was a gentleman. But people loved to gossip, she supposed. She ought to be used to it by now, but it wasn't something that she'd ever get used to. She quickened her steps and caught up with Juan.

"I appreciate everything you've done, Juan, but you know I can't stay here. What would your ma and pa say? They wouldn't like it one bit, and I don't want them embarrassed in front of the whole town. I think it best if Brent and I stayed out in the barn." She swallowed hard. Juan didn't look happy. His lips formed a straight line. He probably had plenty to say but didn't want to in front of Brent.

Juan kept walking. "Let's get you inside and get you warm. Brent, here looks awfully sleepy. We'll talk while he naps."

"Papa, no nap!" Brent shook his head and started tapping the side of Juan's face with his little hand.

Juan's lips curved upward. At least Brent could make him smile. It probably wasn't right that she balk at the arrangement since he gave up his precious horse for her. There was only one bedroom in Juan's house, and her stomach began to turn as she thought about it. Juan had always been a gentleman, but would he stay a gentleman now that he'd rescued her?

When they reached his house, Juan slid the saddle down off his shoulder and set it on the ground. Then he opened the door and carried Brent into his house.

Sonia followed, but her body grew more overwrought with every step. Her whole life she'd been at the mercy of the men in her family. Women didn't seem to matter since they were only good for the work they could do. Once a woman disappointed them, they felt it their right to either throw her out or hit her.

Juan was gentle as he lay Brent down on the bed. He pulled the covers up over him, ruffled his hair a bit, and then kissed him on the cheek.

Juan was a lot like Smitty. Her body began to relax but her stomach still felt as though masses of butterflies were flying in it. She spotted the fresh bread on the counter and smiled. Mercy must have stopped over while Juan was away. She was a good soul and so friendly. Sonia had never felt one ounce of judgment from Mercy.

She grabbed a knife off the counter and began to slice the bread. At the sound of his boots and spurs hitting the wooden floor, her hands faltered, and then she felt the heat of him behind her. He made her feel so safe, but she didn't know if she could trust her feelings or not. Better not to acknowledge him. She set the knife aside and built up the fire in the cook stove. Then she put coffee on to boil.

"Sonia?" he said softly. When she didn't answer he gently touched her shoulders and turned her toward him so that she was in the circle of his arms. He pulled her forward until she hid her face in the crook of his neck as he rubbed her back up and down, gently, the way she'd seen him do with Brent.

She wanted to cry, but she couldn't. She was cried out. Besides his bandanna was wet from all her crying earlier. What he must think of her. It felt so good to be in his arms that her heart began to race and she hoped he couldn't feel it as it thumped hard against her chest. He smelled like leather and horses and soap. She never wanted to let go of him but they needed to talk.

Slowly she drew away from him and looked into his eyes. She wasn't sure what she expected to see. But she didn't expect the kind understanding that she found in them. It was so different from the way he looked at her at the end of the party. Did he feel sorry for her? Did he feel as though she was his responsibility somehow? Did he think of her as weak and pathetic? It was all too much. She walked to the window and gazed at the horses outside in the corral.

"You sure did get a lot of horses. They're beautiful creatures. They look so wild. Are you sure you can break them?"

Juan went to the window and gazed out with her. "That's what I do best. It's been my dream for a long time and I do believe I can make money at it. There are plenty of horses out there but not as prime as these. And it's not easy for the Army to find a Mustang that's saddle broke."

"So you and Greg are doing this together?"

"That's the plan until Carlos is a little older. I'll have to add on to the cabin since he'll probably be living here with me. He snuck out and came with me when I went to capture these last horses." He grimaced. "Not his brightest move, but it turned out fine. I just don't like the fact that he had Ma and Pa worried. I guess he left them a note when he left."

Heat rushed to her face as she turned toward Juan. "I did the same thing. I left them a note when I left. It was cowardly, but I was so afraid they'd try to talk me out of it. I just couldn't ruin their reputations anymore. They didn't deserve it. Your parents are the kindest most decent people I have ever known."

Juan turned toward her and grasped her hand entwining his fingers with hers. "So they had to worry about you two—wait, actually three."

"I figured they'd worry for about a day and then forget about me and Brent." She stared at the floor as she shifted her weight from one foot to the other.

"You're not the type of person that people forget. Plus you have a son. I'm sure they worried the whole time. But here you are safe and sound, and I, for one, am happy." He sighed heavily. "I spent most of the day hunting you down, and I made the mistake of stopping in to see your parents. They've always let me know they have no use for a Mexican and today was no different."

"They go to church every Sunday and sit up front, but they are the most judgmental people I know. They have no tolerance for anyone who's different from them. It's almost as though they don't have opinions of their own but they take the opinions of the wealthier customers and make them theirs. The pastor even came to the house and tried to counsel my parents about helping me, but they refused to change their minds. They kicked me out that very day." She tried to summon a smile but knew she failed.

"Well, it's a good thing you're not like your parents." He

pulled her hand until she followed him to the settee and then he pulled her down next to him. "I guess we need to talk."

Silence fell, and Sonia waited for Juan to start, but it became obvious that she was the one who would have to lead the conversation. She wasn't sure where she wanted to start. She took a deep breath and let it out slowly before she turned and met his gaze.

"I'm sorry that Brent called you Papa. I know it's something you don't want, but I never mentioned it to him because I never planned to see you again. Not that he'd understand anyway he's still too young. In a lot of ways I didn't understand either. I won't lie, you cut me to the core, but the more I thought about it, the more I realized you didn't want to be saddled with a child that wasn't yours. I don't suppose any man does except for Smitty. And he knew going in to his relationship with Lynn that he'd have to take on those kids as his own like he did for you and Carlos. But don't worry, I don't expect it of you. The next time he calls you Papa I'll explain to him that you're not his papa." Sonia bit her lip and looked away. She didn't want to see the satisfaction on his face; it was easier to pretend he'd made a mistake.

"I don't know why I said that. Actually, I take that back. I do know why I said it. I said it because you were getting too close to me, and anyone associated with me ends up tainted. I knew I couldn't be friends with you, so I pushed you away. I just wish I hadn't been so cruel about it." He gave her hand a light squeeze.

"All I can offer is the shame that follows me everywhere. And that was made so clear at the party. I just couldn't take anymore and I left."

"Was the peddler older than you?"

She snapped her head up and stared at him. "Yes, yes he was. He seemed to know the right things to say to me. I guess he sensed my unhappiness with my parents and he used it to make me believe that he would take me away from it all. I played right into his hands, the fool I am. I kept saying no, no, we have to wait until we're married but he had so many reasons why the answer should be yes. I believed him. I believed every single word he said, and there wasn't one that was true. I was devastated when I found that he'd left, and then when I realized I was with child, I'd never been so scared in my life."

"It must've been hard telling your parents. You're a strong courageous woman, Sonia. That peddler took advantage of you. How old are you now?"

"I just turned eighteen. I was fifteen, well almost sixteen years old when he did that to me. I thought I was old enough. I thought my parents were holding me back from becoming an adult, but all they wanted to do was protect me." She studied his face, and although he tried to look expressionless there was a telling twitch of his jaw. He was angry and he had every right to be. She should have said no.

Juan was quiet for a while, and then he released her hand. Next, he stood, went to the stove and poured them both some coffee. He seemed to be taking his time finding words to say, and she didn't blame him. He probably didn't want to talk to her anymore. He handed her the coffee and sat back down beside her.

He slowly took a sip of the steaming brew and then put the cup on the table. "Sonia, you were only fifteen years old. It's not your fault, I think at that age we're all reckless at some point. I know not too long ago I was chafing at the bit to have my own place, and once I got it, I missed home. I missed my brothers and sisters and my ma and pa. I missed all the noisy laughter and loud fights. I thought I wanted quiet and solitude. I was convinced that's what I wanted. But all I found was a lonely existence.

JUAN

I work with Greg every day, and I see Mercy every once in a while, but it's the time right after you eat supper and the dishes are done when you find out how alone you really are. There's no one to share your achievements or your failures with. There's no one to laugh with you over something that happened that day. It's just me staring into the fire knowing that this is the best that it gets. I don't allow myself to dream much further than having a successful horse ranch. There's no sense, I'll never have a wife or children. I imagine many years from now it will just be me and Carlos staring into that same fire."

She couldn't help but stare back. She'd never seen Juan look so vulnerable. Loneliness was a powerful emotion. It was one that she could identify with, and she knew how much it hurt. Even when she had been married, she'd had no one to talk to. She reached up and touched her short hair and frowned.

"I never did ask why you cut your hair so short. Don't get me wrong, it looks fetching on you, but for someone that doesn't want to stick out in the crowd I wouldn't think you would cut it."

She stared into the fire, not wanting to remember. "Roger knew I was pregnant before he married me. That was the very reason why we got married. He went into town the day after we got married stayed at the saloon most of the day and came home mad as a nest o' hornets. He grabbed me by my hair and told me I was an embarrassment to him. I screamed when he backhanded me a few times. Then he took out his big hunting knife and began to saw away my locks. It hurt... His knife wasn't very sharp, but somehow that was my fault too. Then he said no one would ever want to look at me again. After that he fell into bed and slept until the next afternoon while I cried the whole night through. That was my introduction to married life." She clenched and unclenched her hands and finally clasped them together and put them on her lap. She shivered remembering that awful night, but that hadn't been the worst night.

"He was a mean drunk. I've seen many of those in my time, and they find the weakest to pick on. The way your hair curls show your face is pretty."

"You don't have to say that." She reached up and ran her fingers through her hair. "It's grown a bit since then but my hair is slow growing. He had it shorter than a boy's haircut. Of course I didn't leave the house for weeks, and I don't think anyone saw me until Brent was born. Roger was so cheap he didn't want to get the doctor when I was in labor. He said something about women having had babies for thousands of years without doctors. It wasn't until two days later when I was so worn out and I knew I was going to die that he went to town and brought the doctor back with him."

Juan put his arm around her and pulled her close to him until she leaned her head on his shoulder. "You've had a hard time of it. Stay here with me, and I'll keep you safe. No one will harm you while you're with me."

Her heart beat faster, and her mind began to race. She nodded and smiled. "Yes, I would love to marry you." She put her arms around his neck and hugged him.

In her relief she didn't realize that he was trying to set her away from him. When she did take notice her face heated and she knew herself a fool. Looking into Juan's eyes he didn't look back at her. What had just happened?

Juan cleared his throat and shifted even farther away from her. "I can't marry you. I'm sorry if I gave you the wrong impression. I said it all wrong. I want you and Brent to make your home here with me. I'll treat Brent as my own and you'll never have to worry about being hit again or where your next meal would come from. I think we make a good team." It was his turn to blush and it only made her feel worse.

She'd never have another offer from anyone. She tried living on her own, but she couldn't make it. Being part of the team would be better than nothing. Disappointment ran through her. She couldn't blame him for not wanting to marry her. After all she was a fallen woman with a child that everyone knew wasn't her husband's. She drew in a shaky breath and let it back out very slowly. She'd gotten her hopes up once again only to have them dashed.

"I'd be honored to take you up on your generous offer, Juan. Thank you. What about when Carlos comes to live with you in a few years? Will you want us to leave?"

Juan shook his head. He looked decidedly uncomfortable. "This will be your home, and no I would never ask you to leave. It will be nice to have a close friend, and I've become attached to that little guy of yours."

She tilted her head as she tried to read them. "You're not making this offer because you feel sorry for me, are you? I just don't want to be your problem. Brent can you think you're his daddy and I bet there's a multitude of problems we haven't even thought of yet. And I know I've mentioned this before, but I don't think your parents will be happy about this."

Juan took her hand and gave it a squeeze before letting it go. He gave her a real smile, and he seemed to relax. "Let's not borrow trouble. We'll deal with the problems as they arise. It's getting late, and I think we need our sleep. You take the bed with Brent and I'll sleep out here. I think it's time to expand the house. I was going to do it anyway with Carlos coming to live here, but now's just as good a time as any."

Her nerves were frayed, and her whole body felt heavy with exhaustion. She nodded, stood and then headed toward the bedroom. At the bedroom door, she turned. "Good night,

Juan, and thank you." She walked into the room and closed the door behind her.

JUAN WOKE up before the sun rose and built up the fire in the cook stove. He put the coffee on to boil and then sat in a chair at the table. Maybe Sonia was right worrying about what others would think, say, or do. It wasn't going to be easy at first, but people would just have to understand. It wasn't as though they were lying together, but he knew others would believe it. He'd learned to ignore what most people thought, but he was afraid for Sonia. He sighed. He'd made the best decision for their predicament and that was that.

He got up and poured himself a cup of coffee and as he put it on the table, Brent came crawling out of the bedroom straight at him. Juan squatted down just in time to catch the boy as he threw himself at him. It was nice to see such a smile in the morning.

"Papa, me Brent." Then he babbled and Juan had no idea what he was talking about.

"Brent, are you hungry?"

Brent nodded vigorously. "Me hungry, Papa."

There was a feeling of rightness that Juan had never experienced before when Brent wrapped his little arms around his neck and said, "Love you, Papa." Unshed tears stung Juan's eyes. He never expected to have a child in his life. People were too cruel, and he didn't want to have a son or daughter who would have to endure torments for the rest of his or her life.

At the sound of rustling, Juan instantly looked up and met Sonia's gaze. She seemed uneasy and a little bit afraid. Darn her dead husband for making her feel this way. He stood with Brent in his arms and smiled at her. "I think this is the best good morning I've ever had. It's usually so quiet in here in."

"I'm—we—I'm sorry if we disturbed you. We can stay in the bedroom until after you leave in the mornings if you like."

She was a woman with much courage, yet she had many fears. Juan watched as she walked toward them. Her hair stuck up, and he wanted to tease her about it, but he wasn't sure how she would take it.

"I can take him," she put her arms out.

"I tell you what. I'll keep Brent busy if you make breakfast? I'm not much of a cook. Let me know what we need from town, and Greg can get it next time he goes."

She gave him an odd look.

He offered a half shrug. "I don't go into town, and I definitely don't go into your parents' store. It's not worth the aggravation, and it stirs up too much anger inside me. I like it here on the ranch where people know me and don't think of me as different."

"I don't blame you. I don't like to go to town unless I have to. I'm nervous the whole time that someone is going to call me a name. It's bad enough they whisper behind their hands and then look at me. I can hear what they're saying, and they know it. So if Greg is willing, I'd be happy to give you a list." She stood on tiptoe and leaned in, giving Brent a kiss on his cheek.

The sweet smell of her had Juan suddenly wanting things he couldn't have. "I'll take Brent outside to see the horses. Call us when breakfast is ready?"

"Yes I'll call you. Brent you be a good boy for Juan."

Brent shook his head and pursed his lips. "Papa no Juan." He patted Juan's face a few times with his hand. And then he looked at her with his most stubborn look. "Papa."

Juan laughed and hugged Brent tighter. "You're right, Brent, I'm your papa." He carried Brent out the door as her mouth dropped open.

Sonia closed her mouth and shook her head. She immediately went to the window and watched Juan and Brent. She was about to turn around when she spotted Greg heading to the corral. He looked angry. He said something and then turned back without waiting for an answer, stomping to his house. What was that all about? Her heart sank. She had an inkling. No good would come from her staying here, yet she didn't know where else to go.

She quickly fried up some ham while her biscuits baked. As soon as they were done she scrambled some eggs and put everything on platters. She opened the front door and yelled for them to come in for breakfast. Juan smiled at her, and any other time she'd be thrilled, but not today.

They came in and sat down as she put the platters on the wooden table. She then dished out some food for Brent. "Shall we say grace?"

Juan gave her an odd look but he bowed his head as she thanked God for the food and shelter they had been given. Juan fixed his own plate while she helped Brent to navigate eating with a spoon. Most of it ended up on the floor but Brent didn't care. When she finally fixed a plate for herself, Brent got on his knees and tried to put his spoon in her food.

It would have been a perfect time to teach manners, but when he tried to feed her she couldn't help but laugh. He was just trying to help her as she had helped him. Her emotions couldn't take anymore. One minute she was laughing and the next she was extremely upset. It was wearing her out.

She shyly glanced at Juan a few times, and when he gazed

back, she quickly looked down at her plate. Finally she got up her courage to ask. "What was that with Greg? It was about me wasn't it?"

Juan pushed the remaining food on his plate around then put his fork down. "He wanted me to make sure Brent didn't get in the way. For Brent's safety, of course."

"Of course." She didn't believe him. Greg was not pleased she was here. "Look, I don't want to cause you any trouble."

"Sonia, look at me. We're not doing anything wrong. As far as I'm concerned, you work for me and that's that. It's no one's business. Besides, many people have someone to cook and clean for them. It doesn't mean there are feelings involved or anything else is going on."

A knife to her chest would have felt better. "You'll probably have to explain it over and over as everyone asks. Maybe you should ask to see if Carlos can live here too. Then people wouldn't talk so much."

"Carlos needs to finish his education. If he's with me he'll think he can get away with anything he wants. A few more years under Ma and Pa's guidance is what's best for him." He stood and grabbed his hat. "Thank you for breakfast. Make a list if you have a chance, and Greg will go to town. I'll be back a little after noon for something to eat." He hesitated as though he wanted to say more, but in the end, he put on his hat and left. The sound of his boots and spurs grew fainter as he walked down the steps and onto the dirt.

"Let's get you cleaned up." She wet a cloth and washed Brent's face. When she was done she set him on the floor with a wooden bowl and spoon to play with. He liked to make music and it kept him busy.

Cleaning up was easy enough, but she frowned when she looked at the floor. It was scratched and gouged by Juan's spurs. Even sanding it down wouldn't get the deeper gouges gone. But she could keep it clean. She grabbed a broom and did her best.

Laundry needed to be done. She grabbed down the big washtub that hung on the wall and brought it outside. She quickly checked on Brent and then lit a fire in the outside pit. Next she went to the nearby creek and filled two buckets with water. After carrying them back she poured the water into the tub.

The laundry needed to be brought outside as well as Brent. She could still hear him pounding away at the bowl. It was when there was no noise she'd worry. She brought the dirty clothes out first and then Brent. He fussed when he had to leave his bowl inside. The loud sound could disturb the horses but she let him take the spoon with him.

After adding lye soap to the water, she then added the clothes. With a big paddle, she stirred them. Next, she'd need some cold water. She lifted Brent up into her arms and grabbed hold of one bucket. She'd need to make a few trips. On her second trip, Greg came and carried the bucket for her.

Her heart thumped as soon as she saw him. She wasn't ready to hear what he had to say. If one more person told her she wasn't welcome, she knew she'd break down. If it was just her, it would be bearable, but she had Brent to consider.

They walked to the creek in silence and as soon as they got there he stopped and turned toward her. "We have a ranch to build. No one is better with horses than Juan, and I don't want him hurt."

"I don't plan to hurt him—"

He put up his hand to silence her. "You might not plan to but you already are. Do you think anyone will buy horses from us when they know you're living with Juan? It might have been a tough sale with Juan being Mexican, but some believe they are good with horses. I can't make excuses or explain why you're here. The whole town will know soon enough and while we do have an Army order, we'll need more sales than that to grow larger. I'm not trying to be mean. I know you're a good person and Juan is crazy about you but I'm just telling you the way of it. Living here and working for him will be seen as a sin by some people."

"I can get the water myself," she whispered. "I understand, just please go." She grabbed the bucket from him and with one hand she filled it. Brent thought touching the water fun and he cooed loudly. When she turned back to the path, Greg was gone.

A tear rolled down her face. She thought Greg would be on Juan's side. Perhaps warning her away was protecting Juan. No matter, she needed to find another solution, and it wouldn't be anywhere close.

She dashed away her tear and carried the bucket and Brent back to the wash. She set Brent down so he could dig in the dirt while she rinsed and wrung out the clothes. It was a lengthy process that she'd had to do when she lived with her parents. Doing it for people who appreciated it somehow made it different. It wasn't the world's worst chore; it was something she didn't mind doing for the people she cared about.

Her stomach clenched and twisted as she thought about Greg's speech. He was right. She did need to leave Juan alone. Soon enough he'd realize his mistake and then he'd feel bound to provide them with shelter. Certainly his parents wouldn't agree with the relationship.

She'd finished wringing out the last item of clothing when she noticed that Brent was gone. Fear filled her as she looked around the house. He wasn't there. Next she checked the barn and there he was crawling around, following Juan.

She closed her eyes for a moment and sighed. Then she quickly whisked Brent up and began to hurry away.

"He crawled all this way!" Juan said with excitement in his voice.

"Well he's pretty fast at it. I'm sorry he got in your way." She didn't wait for a reply. Instead she hurried to the house. She was going to miss him something fierce.

"It's naptime little one. I can't believe you crawled to the barn. You've made such strides in the last month. I'm very proud of you." She set him down on the bed and put a pillow next to him in case he suddenly rolled over. He settled down quickly, and his eyes closed. Quietly, she slipped out and closed the door.

She quickly sliced the ham and put it inside the cut open biscuit. She made six of them hoping it was enough for Juan to eat. Then she hurried outside and began to hang the wash up on the clothesline.

From behind, she heard footsteps coming toward her and she stiffened, knowing it was Juan.

"Coming in to eat?" he asked.

She didn't look at him. "No, I'm not all that hungry, but I fixed you something." She could feel the heat of his eyes on her, but she made herself stand with her back to him. He stood there for what seemed like forever before she heard the thud of his boots and the jingle of his spurs. She didn't relax until he was inside the house.

He was in there for a while, and she was glad he didn't expect to talk to her. It must be time for him to go back to work. She waited, but he was still in the house. When she was done hanging clothes, she cleaned out the big tub, put out the fire, and stacked everything that needed to go back into the house by the steps. Then she sat down.

She'd sit until he went back to work or Brent woke up.

"I need to talk to you," Juan said.

Startled, she jumped. She hadn't heard the door open. She might as well face him. He knew she had to go just as much as she did. She stood and turned. He was no longer at the open door. She climbed the steps and went inside then closed the door behind her.

There he stood, staring at her. He looked her up and down, taking her all in, and it made her nervous. He stared at her again with a look of need in his eyes. He took a big step toward her and ended up so close he almost touched her.

"Juan–"

He lowered his head and kissed her. It was almost as though she'd never been kissed before. She felt excitement throughout her whole body, and it felt right. He lifted his head and stared into her eyes. What he saw she had no idea but he pulled her toward him and held her close, rocking her from side to side. He stroked her back, telling her it would be fine.

He was one of the few who'd ever tried to comfort her, and it wasn't long before the tears started. Almost no one else had ever bothered to try to help her or make her feel better. Swallowing hard, she blinked until she stopped her tears and pulled back until he let her go.

"I already know. It's goodbye. I'll be out of your house as soon as I can."

His brown eyes grew wide. "What are you talking about? You're not leaving."

She stared at the floor. "I would never allow anything to get in the way of your dream or your success. You're going to have a big horse ranch, and I know people will come from all over just to buy horses you trained."

"What has that got to do with you leaving?" He put his finger under her chin and lifted her face until she looked at him.

"It's just common sense. No one will buy from you if they know I'm here." She didn't want to talk about it anymore.

"I already have contracts for the next two years. I can

provide for you and Brent." He gazed at her, and he scowled. "What's the real reason you're leaving?"

"I don't want to tell you."

"What did Greg say to you?" His voice started getting louder.

"Shh, don't wake Brent. Juan, he has your best interest at heart. It's better I leave as soon as I can make arrangements. You're the best man, I know and I don't want to have my heart ripped out if I stay only to have you turn me away. I—"

He moved quickly and took her into his embrace again. She could feel the strength of his arms and the hardness of his muscled chest. She trembled as he kissed her again. This time the kiss was much longer and deeper, and she should have pushed him away again, but she wanted to have this memory of him.

They were both breathing hard when he finally stepped back.

"You don't want to leave. I can feel it."

"You might be right, but life isn't about what we want. It's about what we must do. I refuse to be held responsible when your dreams start to crumble. It's Greg's dream too. He makes a lot of sense."

"Sonia, Greg is richer than—well he's loaded. The ranch will grow."

She shook her head. "You wouldn't take money from Greg if the horses weren't selling. It's for the best, Juan."

He glanced away and then gave her a hardened look. "It's because I'm Mexican. You're afraid we'll end up being intimate, and you'll end up with a part Mexican baby." He breathed out loudly as pain flashed in his eyes. "I understand." He turned and walked out the door.

He never gave her a chance to deny it. *God please help me, help us. I know I have to leave. I just don't want him thinking I'd judge him because his skin is different from mine.*

JUAN

She needed to stay busy. She tidied up the papers Juan had. It looked as though he hadn't had time to read them. The local periodical usually was full of gossip, and she didn't need to read about how much people despised her. She turned one over and saw ads placed on the back page. Ads for mail order brides.

She instantly sat down and read a few. Most wanted a God-fearing woman who knew about farm work or ranch work. She was in the age range many posted. Perhaps if she wrote them all, she'd get lucky with a marriage proposal.

She found paper and a pencil and sat at the table writing to the men. Would having a son disqualify her? She hoped not. She addressed each of them. Greg was going to town in the morning. He'd probably be more than happy to send her letters out.

THE NEXT DAY Juan went into the house, his heart filled with anger. Greg had had a lot to say about having Sonia living with him. Greg thought they should marry since no one with eyes would believe she was just the help. When had Greg become so pious? Juan bit his tongue for the most part. How could his brother and friend act this way?

"Did you give Greg the list?" Sonia asked. She looked worried, and it took his anger even higher.

"He'll be leaving in a minute. Was there something else you needed?" He hated that his voice was full of anger too.

"Watch Brent for me!" She sailed out the door without a backward glance at him.

Juan went to the door and watched while Sonia spoke to Greg. He actually seemed happy about something she said. Juan didn't like it one bit, but he wasn't going to take out his anger on Sonia. She'd had enough for a lifetime.

She ran back to the house and smiled at him. "Working with the horses today?"

"I'm going to check on the cattle and see why Journey hasn't come back."

Her brow wrinkled. "What do you mean about Journey?"

"Journey always comes back to me if someone else is riding him. He'll find a moment to slip away from Wendell. I just thought it would have been sooner than later."

Sonia laughed. "You are a sly one, Juan. I'll keep my eye out for him. I have some baking to do. And keeping up with Brent is getting to be a full time job. Too bad I don't have a corral for him to play in."

Her melodious laugh soothed him a bit but he still had plenty of anger in him. "I'll see ya."

"Papa!" Brent crawled awfully fast toward him.

Juan bent down and caught the child, lifting him up and kissing his cheek. "I have work to do, little man, but I'll be back." He went to put him down, but Brent refused to let go. "Brent, I really do need to go."

"Me work." Brent nodded his head and wrapped his arms tightly around Juan's neck.

Sonia patted Brent's back. "Come on, little one, you can help knead the bread."

Brent suddenly let go and turned in Juan's arms so quickly, Juan thought he'd drop him. But he landed safely in his mother's arms.

Juan didn't say anything else. He grabbed his hat and walked out the door. He was disappointed Sonia hadn't apologized to him. She hadn't told him he was wrong about her not wanting a Mexican man or child.

He saddled his buckskin and rode off. Between Sonia and Greg, he didn't feel welcome in his own home. He'd have to find somewhere for her to live. She didn't want to be there. If only he'd known before Greg had had a chance to insult her.

They wouldn't have fought before he left for town. If Mercy hadn't come out, he might have taken a swing at Greg.

Who did he think he was interfering in his personal life? Just because Greg was the oldest and married with a child didn't make him in charge of anything. Maybe a joint venture wasn't a good idea.

The cattle were lowing. There were a few pregnant ones, and he needed to make sure they were healthy. He checked them one by one and they all appeared fine. Next he checked that the access to the creek was clear. One time a tree had come down in a bad storm and the cattle didn't know what to do. Now he always checked. They'd need to drive them to the south pasture before long. If there still was a they.

Hunger pains gnawed at him, but he didn't want to go back to the house. He was still hurt, but he knew he'd end up kissing her again. He never felt more alive than when he was kissing Sonia. But she'd shown her cards, and she was leaving.

He rode and checked on their hay crop, and then he headed back toward the house. There was plenty of daylight left for him to try to break a horse or two.

His house and barn came to view and he almost laughed. Journey was wandering around outside the barn, apparently looking for some grain. Relief filled Juan that his horse was back. Wendell could go to the sheriff but trading a horse for people wasn't legal. Everyone knew that. He wasn't too concerned that Wendell would come and try to take the horse back. Wendell was a coward and a bully.

Journey trotted out to meet him, and Juan smiled. "I knew you'd be home. I bet you're hungry."

Journey turned and raced to the barn. "He's hungry all right," he said to the buckskin.

As soon as he got to the barn, he jumped down and led Journey into a stall. He filled his trough with grain and made sure he had water before he took care of the buckskin. Then he let himself into Journey's stall and looked him over.

"Looks like you're fine. I was a little worried about Wendell. But it looks like he took care of you. I'm glad you're back."

Journey stopped eating and pushed his head against Juan's shoulder. It was Journey's way of showing affection.

Juan had worked with a Palomino until it was too dark to see. He saw Sonia watching him from the window but he didn't acknowledge her. She had the power to cripple him, and he couldn't allow it. After all he was just a Mexican. A man people hired but didn't befriend or marry. It had been that way all his life, so why it hurt now he didn't know.

He slowly walked to his house and sat on the steps looking at the full moon. Sonia had kissed him as though she desired him. It was like a puzzle he couldn't figure out. One minute she seemed sweet on him, and then she was extremely cold the next.

It was a lonely feeling. He had nowhere else to go. No friends to drop in on. It hadn't mattered to him before. He liked being alone but it would have been nice to talk to someone about everything that was going on. It wasn't something he could talk to Carlos or his parents about. He was a man now. Glancing over at Greg's house, he grew envious. The lights were all on, and he could see Greg and Mercy laughing together. Frowning, Juan stood up and went inside his own place.

Sonia was sitting, sewing. She didn't even look up at him. "Dinner is still warm. I fixed you a plate." She didn't even pause her stitching as she told him. Brent must be asleep already. Too bad; he would have been a good distraction.

Without bothering to thank her, Juan just grabbed his plate and sat at the table. He ate without tasting the food, too intent on watching Sonia to care what he put in his mouth.

The thought of kissing her never left; it just grew stronger. He finished and put his plate on the counter. Grabbing a piece of wood he sat near Sonia. He planned to whittle a set of blocks for Brent to play with.

"What if I promise never to touch you?" he blurted out.

She set her sewing aside and gazed at him. "That wouldn't work. I feel too much inside for you."

"If I had white skin, it wouldn't be a problem though." He couldn't help the bitterness that came through in his voice.

"I don't know why you think that. I never said a word about your heritage."

"You didn't deny it either."

"Juan—."

" I'm too gruff aren't I? Maybe I'm not handsome enough?"

She shook her head. "Juan you are perfect just the way you are. Any woman would be proud to have your attention."

"But not you." He needed to get out of there. Rage, disappointment, and hurt were upon him, and he didn't want to do or say something he'd regret. "You want me to leave you alone. I understand now." He stood, grabbed a few blankets and his hat, and then walked out. The barn was as good as any place to sleep. Could he live in the same house as she? Perhaps it *was* for the best that she leave.

CHAPTER SEVEN

It had been a long three weeks, and Sonia's nerves were frayed. She accepted a proposal from a rancher in a town about six hours away, and she'd be leaving in three days' time. All she needed to do was tell Juan. He'd been as touchy as a bear with a sliver in its paw.

She had finally convinced him to sleep inside the house. The guilt of being warm and comfortable while he slept with the horses grew to be too much. Still, she didn't see him much. He was gone before she wakened and he came home after she went to bed. It had been lonely.

Greg and Mercy had helped her to gather items she'd need for her new life. She hadn't wanted them to spend any money on her, but they'd insisted. Greg was obviously thrilled she was leaving. At least Mercy was nice and understanding, but she never had much advice. She said she hadn't known a thing about men until Greg came into her life.

Juan planned to work close to home today, and Sonia planned to make him listen to her. Mercy had already offered to watch Brent.

It would take all of her courage and strength to go and talk to Juan. She had feelings for him but she had to set aside what she felt and do what was best for everyone. After checking her hair in the mirror one more time she carried Brent over to Mercy. Brent smiled when Mercy took him into her arms, and he didn't look back. Sonia had thought she'd have to leave a crying boy, but he was just as happy without her. Somehow it made her heart squeeze.

Juan was in the corral kicking up dust as he held on to the saddle. The bay he was riding kicked and bucked, but Juan held on. It was a magnificent sight. Finally they began to move as one. She was going to miss him. He already held a big piece of her heart.

She approached quietly, not wanting to spook the horse. When she stood just outside the corral, she waited and watched. Juan acted as though he didn't see her. He turned his back to her more than once, and when he was done with the bay horse, he let it loose in the pasture and then headed into the barn without acknowledging her. It felt as though she'd been gut punched. She had a hard time breathing for a moment.

Maybe she should just walk away. He'd notice when she left for good, she supposed. He'd probably be just as glad to have the house back all to himself. Straightening her shoulders, she lifted her head trying to look confident even though she shook inside. She walked to the barn and entered.

It was a bit dim, but sunlight shone through the doors. Juan was talking to Journey. She'd made enough noise as she scuffled her feet, but he still pretended she wasn't there. Her shoulders sagged, and she stared at the ground. He didn't want to talk to her. She didn't have the strength to force him to talk to her. If only things had been different, she would have worked this ranch with him. Brent was going to miss him. He already did, and it confused him why Papa wasn't around.

A sob she'd been pushing down since she walked into the barn escaped. She turned and ran to the house. He wouldn't follow her; he didn't care.

When she walked into the bedroom, she pulled the valise Lynn had given her out from under the bed. She had a few more items to pack. She didn't need to wait until she talked to him to be ready to leave. She'd do a final wash tomorrow. There would be no goodbye, and maybe that would be best for Brent.

A trickle of awareness crept along her spine, and she felt the heat of Juan's stare on her. "I didn't hear you come in." She didn't look at him, just kept folding things and putting them in the valise.

"Did you need something?" he asked, and his voice was surprisingly gentle.

"No, I'm fine. I don't need anything from you. You've made it obvious that you don't care anyway. Brent and I will be just fine." She swallowed back the lump that was forming in her throat and forced herself to glance up at him. "I found a place to go, and we're leaving in three days." Why did her voice have to quaver? Quickly she looked back down into her valise.

"Are you going to live with my ma and pa?"

"No, I'm going to get married. Now if you'll excuse me, I have more packing to do."

"What do you mean you're getting married?" His voice became louder.

She didn't answer him. She thought she'd been ready to tell him, but she didn't feel courageous anymore, and her strength was depleting fast.

"Sonia, who are you marrying? I haven't seen anyone here courting you."

She couldn't pretend to pack anymore. She'd get a cup of coffee and sit down for a bit. As she walked past Juan he grabbed her arm and prevented her from going any farther.

Automatically, she put her other hand up to protect her face while her body tensed, waiting for the blow that would be coming.

Juan let her go and stepped back. "You thought I'd hit you? You know me better than that." He stared at her, and she noted the confusion in his eyes.

She walked to the cook stove. "Did you want a cup of coffee?"

"Sure. Now why did you think I was going to beat you?"

Her hands shook so badly that Juan took the coffee pot from her and poured two cups. He put them on the kitchen table and then held out a chair for her. He sat across from her.

"I—I'm sorry it's just a reaction. I can't help it. I know you wouldn't hit me but I'd been hit as soon as I'd been grabbed so many times before that I guess my mind went back to it and I automatically needed to protect my face and head. I'm sorry." The hurt on his face became imprinted on her heart.

He nodded, but he frowned. "Who asked you to marry him?"

"A rancher named David Winstone. He's in need of a wife to help with his ranch." She gave him a smile but his eyes narrowed. He didn't appear to believe her smile.

"When did you meet this David Winstone? I don't recall ever hearing that name before." He stared at her making her nervous.

"I haven't yet. I'll be a mail order bride. Many women do it, and it's a perfectly fine way to find a husband. He even said he'd raise Brent as his own. He has horses and cattle like you do. He wants children, and he wants me to share his life."

JUAN

She couldn't summon excitement about the next chapter in her life.

"I see." Juan stood up and left, slamming the door behind him.

Her stomach churned, and she shook as tears began to flow. He didn't care, and here she was wasting her tears on him. But she couldn't help it. She'd forget him soon enough, she supposed. That's what she'd been telling herself, anyway, and now she realized she'd been lying to herself.

She needed to go get Brent. After washing her face, she walked to Greg and Mercy's house and knocked on the door.

Upon answering, Mercy took one look at her and hugged her. "I'm guessing it didn't go well. Both of the children are napping. Come talk to me." Mercy led her back outside and they sat on the wooden chairs on the porch.

"I suppose it went as well as…" She released a heavy sigh. "It was awful. He ignored me the whole time I was at the corral. I followed him into the barn and the same thing happened. A sob I'd been holding in came out, and I turned and hurried back to the house. I've been unwanted plenty of times but it never hurt as much as it did today." She took a deep breath. "I told him I was to be a mail order bride, and he walked out of the house slamming the door."

"Oh, dear."

"Actually it just reinforces that he doesn't want me around. I'm sure I'll have a good life with David Winstone. It'll be nice to be welcomed again."

Mercy nodded. "What did you tell him about Brent's father?"

"I lied and said he was dead." Sonia shook her head. "I hate to start our marriage with a lie between us, but I have to protect Brent and my reputation too."

"I think you did the right thing." Mercy reached over and

patted Sonia's hand. "The men will be branding tomorrow. We won't see much of them in the next few days anyway."

"I suppose it's a good thing."

A soft cry came from inside.

"I hear Hannah, and I bet Brent isn't far behind. Thank you so much for watching him." They stood and Sonia hugged Mercy. "I appreciate the friendship you've extended to me."

"You're easy to like, Sonia." Mercy led the way into the house and the bedroom where the two children had been sleeping. Both women laughed. Hannah was sitting on top of Brent jabbering at him in baby talk. Brent just smiled at Hannah.

"It's a shame you're leaving. I bet these two would have been the best of friends," Mercy commented as she lifted Hannah off of Brent.

"They might have," Sonia answered wistfully. She lifted Brent and carried him to the front door. "Thank you again." She nodded and left.

Heart sore was how she felt. She cared for Juan, she just hadn't known how much. Would she ever feel that way about David Winstone? It didn't really matter of course. He was her future.

Night was falling, and Greg had a roaring fire going. Juan was tired. It had been a long day of rounding up the cattle and then branding them. They had one more day of it, and then they'd head home. Not long after that, Sonia and Brent would leave. He hadn't even asked her how she was getting to her new destination or if she needed anything. He could have offered her some money. He owed her wages, he'd just pay her a generous amount.

JUAN

"Juan!"

"What?"

"I've been talking to you for a full five minutes or so, and now I see you haven't been hearing a word I said." Greg sounded disgusted, but he had a smile on his face. "What's on your mind? Horses?"

"Did you know Sonia is getting married? She doesn't even know the fella. He could be another woman beater for all she knows. Sometimes I wonder if she uses the brain God gave her."

"I knew. In fact I sent out the original eight letters for her. She had three proposals to consider, and she chose Winstone. He seems like a nice enough man." Greg shrugged.

"Tell me what you know that makes him a nice enough man? Would you want Mercy to go off and marry a man who is 'nice enough'? Was this your idea? You hate that Sonia lives with me!" Juan started to stand.

"I'm not going to fight you, so you might as well sit. Sonia has made choices in her life that led to her having no choices. At least she found someone willing to take her and the boy. Someone who is willing to marry her. One of the men wanted her to leave Brent behind because he wasn't willing to raise another man's son. Believe me, Winstone was by far the best of the bunch. She'll be fine."

Juan choked back the bile that rose into his mouth. *The best of the bunch?* What did that even mean? "Were any inquiries made about his character?"

Greg shook his head. "No, if you want to be a mail order bride I guess you pray that you get a good husband." He leaned back against his saddle as though everything was fine.

"Don't you think I'd marry her if she was willing? We both know I can't marry a white woman. I don't suppose I could talk her out of it. I pay her a good wage."

"It's not the same. You know how women are like chickens, they like to nest."

Juan widened his eyes. "Did you just compare Mercy to a chicken?"

"No, not my Mercy. She'd probably want to be the rooster." Greg smiled. "I would have been happy if the two of you got married. Just so you know there's no law keeping you from marrying her."

"She wouldn't have me. I always knew I'd live alone unless a Mexican woman miraculously crossed my path. I tried not to feel anything for her. I always knew this would be the outcome." He shook his head. "I'm going to get some shut-eye," Juan announced as he got comfortable on his bedroll. He put his back to the fire. He wasn't going to get any sleep. How stupid were Greg and Sonia? He tilted his head until he could stare at the stars. There was a big part of him that didn't want Sonia to leave…ever. But she was a grown woman with a child; she could make her own decisions.

He rolled over and stared into the fire, watching the flames lick up toward the sky. She'd been just a child when that peddler had taken advantage of her. She'd probably had very few happy days since then. She hadn't been prepared for people to turn their backs on her.

It was different with him and Carlos. They had known from the first that they were different and people didn't like different. It hurt like hell. He remembered trying to explain it to Carlos after he'd been chased home from school. His throat had burned while he tried to explain the way things were. It didn't make much sense then, and it didn't make sense now.

God made him in his likeness. People told him God was white but in his heart Juan didn't believe that God was one color. Or maybe God intended for everyone to get along despite their differences. What ever happened to God's words, *"This is My commandment, that you love one another, just as I have loved you."* He sighed. This wasn't about him; it was about Sonia. But the same words applied to Sonia too.

She'd made her decision. Heck, she'd even set up a marriage for herself. Would she be safe? What about Brent? Would this David make her happy? Juan wanted nothing more than to see her smile. A real smile that wasn't covering her worries. She deserved that.

He was better for knowing her, but now he'd know loneliness and regret. He'd miss what could have been and what would have been if he'd been born into a different family. He was proud of his heritage, and he needed to remember that.

It was going to be so hard to let her go. Brent would probably call David, Papa. Already Juan's heart hurt, and she wasn't even gone yet.

He shifted, struggling to find comfort on the hard ground. He had a long day tomorrow and he needed to get some shut-eye. Once more, he rolled over, and finally he fell asleep.

SONIA WOKE FEELING MELANCHOLY. She'd be leaving tomorrow. She sat at the table drinking her coffee. Brent had been up a couple times through the night, and this morning he was still sleeping. It was unusual to have such peace and quiet.

A familiar sound drifted in from outside, and she held her breath. It couldn't be! Heart racing, she listened, and indeed it was the clanking of pots and pans knocking against each other on a peddler's wagon. The noise brought back all the bad memories of how stupid she'd been.

She grabbed her shawl and wandered outside. Her

peddler had never been in the area since he'd left her in shame. It had taken a while before she had found the courage to approach any of the other peddler's wagons that had rolled through town. She didn't have money now, but she liked to look and see what wares were on the wagon. As she strode up to the wagon, she eyed the driver, and her breath escaped her, causing her to feel lightheaded.

She sat down on the porch step trying to catch her breath. She glanced at the peddler again, and her heart plummeted as shame enveloped her. It was as though she was fifteen again. It was Arthur Spade, the man who seduced her and left her.

Bitterness rose inside of her and she was tempted to run back into the house, but he saw her. Surprisingly there was no flicker of recognition in his eyes. Just how many girls had he promised to marry that he didn't recall her? Hopefully, most weren't as stupid as she and not every girl he tried to seduce had jumped the gun anticipating her wedding night.

He hopped down off his wagon. His suit was in tatters. She'd never noticed before that he was so poorly dressed. He was still a handsome devil though. He smiled and now with experience behind her she could easily tell it was insincere.

He took off his hat and waved it in front of him as he bowed to her. "Good morning, lovely lady. I'm presuming you're the lady of the house." He stood up straight and flashed another smile. He looked puzzled when she didn't smile back.

She had to bite her tongue. She was so tempted to tell him exactly how he ruined her life but he must not find out about Brent. He might try to take him. She grew increasing cold at the thought. "I'm just visiting."

"How fortuitous that we have met; I'm visiting too. We are like fellow travelers. Perhaps you'd like to pick out something for free? I couldn't allow such a beautiful woman as you go without." He winked at her.

She wanted to be sick. "Actually I think I hear my child awake. Good day."

"I'll be camping here tonight. Eli Todd gave me permission."

"This isn't Eli's land. It's not mine either." She hurried inside, closed the door, and pressed her back against it. What was she to do? Eli must have meant another piece of land but of course there would be no one to sell to.

Her hands shook as she barred the door. She and Brent could spend the day inside. She'd often wished to see Arthur again so she could beat him with one of the cast iron pans he sold. But now that he was here, she dared not. It just wouldn't be safe.

She heard Brent's cries and hurried into the bedroom to get him up. She got him dressed and then sat him on a chair in the kitchen so he could watch her make breakfast. After he ate, she put him on the floor. He crawled around and then crowed.

Sonia hurried over and saw that Juan had finished making the blocks for her son. He was beyond excited to have the blocks. She showed him how to stack them and then knock them down. He laughed and laughed every time they fell.

"I have to clean the kitchen. You build now." She kept an eye on him as she cleaned. Brent was good at stacking the blocks and even better at knocking them over. She'd have to remember to thank Juan when he got back.

Her heart jumped into her throat. Oh no! What would Juan say when he saw the peddler?

The knock at the door did nothing to calm her nerves. "Who is it?"

"It's me, Mercy."

Sonia opened the door only wide enough for Mercy to get in and then closed and barred it.

"What in the world?" Mercy raised her eyebrows.

"That's him. That's the peddler that, well he, well—"

"The one who caused you so much heartache?" Mercy gave her a sad smile when she nodded. "Did you talk to him?"

"I did, and he didn't recognize me. I've decided to stay inside all day. I can't have him suddenly remember and want to take Brent. He'll be gone tomorrow."

"So will you," Mercy said sadly. "I have to get back to Hannah. She was so cranky last night. Neither of us got much sleep. I'll try to come back over with her later."

Sonia unbarred the door, opened it so Mercy could get out, and then closed and barred it once again. It was a bit sad. She was just getting to know Mercy. Hopefully there would be a lot of friends to make at her new home.

Would her new husband's ranch be big? He'd written that he had both cattle and horses but had not said which was his main focus. Would it be cattle or horses? Hopefully the house was well built. She'd find out soon enough. Looking around Juan's cabin, though, she knew she'd miss it and Juan as well.

There wasn't much to do. She was packed and she had a stew on. She sat on the floor and played blocks with Brent. She showed him how to put them in a row like a wagon train and how to make them look like a square corral. He repeated every word after her and pride filled her.

Brent started to get tired, but he refused to nap. It was late afternoon, and he just cried and cried. Perhaps it was the last of his teeth coming in? She just didn't know. He didn't have a fever or rash. Finally after what seemed like hours his eyes closed.

She couldn't stand it anymore; she needed some fresh air. Arthur hadn't recognized her earlier anyway. Maybe it would be safe.

She poured herself some coffee and headed out to sit on the porch. As soon as she sat, she sighed. Hopefully Brent would be fine on the journey they were to take in the morning. It would be stressful as it was. Looking around, she saw no sign of Arthur. Maybe he was at the creek. She didn't care as long as he left her alone.

He rounded the corner of Juan's house and startled her.

"Having a nice day?" he asked.

"Not too bad."

"I heard your little one crying. Is there anything I can do? I have a few toys on my wagon."

"No, thank you anyway. Juan whittled him a set of blocks, and we've been playing with them." She kept her gazes at a minimum.

"Is he your husband?"

"No, he's just a friend. He's been kind to me and my son since my husband died." She glanced at him quickly and saw his eyes narrow.

She stood. "It's been nice chatting with you, but I must get back inside."

Arthur was quick. He got to the door before she even knew what was happening. "I remember you, Sonia," he whispered in her ear.

She turned and sat back down. There was no way she'd allow him inside. "You must be thinking of someone else."

"I don't think so. A man doesn't forget a willing little thing like you. Too bad I couldn't have stayed in town longer. It was good between us. So who is Juan? Is he the Mexican who lives out this way?" He inched closer to her, and her heart began to thump against her chest.

"Like I said, he's a friend."

Arthur sneered. "I bet you've had many 'friends' since I left. Your mother was so hoity-toity with her nose so far in the air. It felt *goo-ood* to take her daughter. I bet it knocked her down a peg or two." He laughed, a sickening chuckle without humor.

"Is that what the whole seduction was about? To get at my mother? You led me into hell and left me there because my mother slighted you? What kind of man are you? Never mind, don't answer. I already know." She pushed up from the chair and tried to dash around him but he caught her around the waist. She pushed and kicked and finally clawed his face with her fingernails.

Arthur was able to get the door open, and he hauled her inside. He slapped her so hard across the face she went flying until she hit the floor. "I expect you to behave. Besides I've already had you. You're a fallen woman, Sonia. You belong in a brothel."

She sat up and touched her head. There was blood on her fingers. "I might have been a fallen little girl, but I confessed my sins and asked God for forgiveness. There are second chances, and my past doesn't have to pull me down to your level."

"I suppose you have morals now too, eh? Sonia, that's not how it works at all. Once fallen…that's it."

She stood and faced him. "If we confess our sins, He is faithful and just to forgive us our sins and to cleanse us from all unrighteousness."

"You believe what you want. Makes no never mind to me as long as I get what I want."

Brent started wailing and she hurried to get him. He was still fussing. She carried him to the kitchen. "I need to feed him."

Arthur's jaw dropped. "He's mine. What's wrong with him? Was he born slow?"

"He is the perfect child."

Arthur scratched his chin. "Then you must baby him too much. Does he walk?"

"Not yet." She kept her gaze on Brent as she tried to give

him a bit of the stew. Let him think there was something wrong. Maybe he'd just leave.

"You know what I think? I think this Juan isn't coming back tonight. No one likes to ride at night and it's getting dark. You are just full of lies aren't you? Maybe I should take you with me in the morning. You can lie to the customers and tell them how wonderful my goods are. They might even buy more if I have a family with me." Arthur slapped his hand down on the table. "By golly, I think it's a fine idea."

Sonia tried to ignore him. Of course Juan would be here, wouldn't he? But what if—? Maybe he was waiting until she left. Suddenly she was scared.

The door flew open so hard it hit the wall, and Juan walked in with his rifle ready to shoot. "Hold it right there. Don't make a move." He glared at Arthur. "Honey, I want you and Brent over here with me."

Tears pricked at the back of her eyes as relief surged through her. She picked up Brent, who started to cry again and then she hurried and stood right next to Juan.

He looked her over and frowned when he looked at her head. "You all right?"

"Now that you're here I am."

"Want you to go over to Greg's house. Mercy was on her way here with a rifle when we rode up." He kept the rifle trained on Arthur while he ushered both Sonia and Brent outside.

Greg and Mercy both were there on the front porch with rifles.

"Mercy, take them home. I'll be there as soon as we get rid of that piece of garbage," Greg said.

Clutching a squirming Brent close against her chest, Sonia stumbled next to Mercy. She couldn't get away from Arthur fast enough.

After they were inside Greg and Mercy's house, Sonia

finally broke down. Tears rolled down her face. "I don't know what I would have done if you hadn't shown up."

"I knew something was wrong," said Mercy. I just couldn't shake the feeling. Come on, now. Let's sit. You and Brent are safe."

Sonia blinked away her tears and looked around. At the sight of Hannah sitting in the middle of what looked like a miniature corral, she gasped. "I was just telling Juan I needed one of those."

"Yes, I know." Mercy nodded. "He told Greg, who decided to make me one. It's the best idea ever. Go on and put Brent in it with her."

Brent was still crying until Sonia set him down. He instantly smiled at Hannah, and she smiled back.

Sonia laughed and cried at the same time. "He's been crying all day. I should have borrowed Hannah."

"Come, sit. I want to look at your head." Mercy grabbed a bowl of water and a towel.

Sonia sat and wiped her tears. She winced and tried to keep from flinching away as Mercy doctored her.

Greg opened the door to his cabin but Juan went through it first. He quickly glanced around until he saw Sonia. He immediately went to her and squatted down before her.

He cupped her chin gently and turned her head this way then that way. "Are you hurt anywhere else? That looks bad."

"It was worse before Mercy tended to it, and I'm fine. I'm not sure what my new husband will think when he sees the cut and bruise on my forehead." She stared over his head as though she was unable to meet his gaze.

"You'll have to postpone going to him, I guess," Juan said as hope grew in his heart.

JUAN

"Unfortunately, that won't do. Greg made all the arrangements for me to get there." She lowered her gaze until she met his, and she cringed. He must look as mad as he felt.

He stood up and then stood toe to toe with Greg. "Would you like to explain any of this?" There was no mistaking the anger in his voice.

"I'm sorry, Juan. At the time I thought I was doing you a favor."

Juan nodded and stepped away. "I'm tired. Are you and Brent coming, Sonia?"

She readily nodded. "It's time we left Mercy to a bit of peace. What did you do to Arthur?"

"He's tied up in the barn." Greg smiled at their accomplishment.

Mercy snickered. "No better place for a varmint like him."

Sonia stared, mouth gaping. She looked like she wanted to say something, but in the end, just shook her head. "Goodnight. Thank you both for all your help." She held her arms down into the miniature corral and tried to get Brent but he scooted to the far side. She went around to catch him, but he moved again and stared her down wearing his mulish expression.

Juan walked over and Brent cooed in delight. "Papa!" he said as he crawled toward Juan. Then Brent grabbed on to the side of the corral and pulled himself up to a standing position. He looked so pleased with himself.

"Well, look at you standing there like a big boy. Come on, let Papa carry you home."

Brent went willingly into Juan's arms and patted his face with his little hand again. Brent made him feel as though he was ten feet tall.

"We'll see you in the morning," Juan said as he escorted Sonia and Brent out the door. He didn't say a word until they entered his house.

He still held Brent but he turned his head and caught Sonia's glance. "We have a lot to talk about tonight."

"Yes, I suppose we do as it's my last. I'll put Brent down."

Juan shook his head. "Let me. I want to remember everything about this young boy who calls me Papa. I'm going to miss him more than I ever imagined."

Sonia nodded.

Juan took his time getting Brent changed and tucking him in. He sat on the side of the bed and stared at him, wanting to remember everything about him. He'd never be a father to any other child, and emptiness filled his heart. Leaning over he kissed Brent's cheek.

Brent gave a contented smile as he closed his eyes.

Juan took a deep fortifying breath before he had to try to talk Sonia out of going. He had no idea how it would go.

She looked up at him as he entered the room and smiled hesitantly.

He smiled back and sat next to her on the settee. "Are you sure you're all right? When did that loser show up?"

Her lips twitched when he said loser. "He was here right before sunrise. I heard the clatter of the pots on the wagon before it drove up. I didn't realize it was him until I went outside, but he didn't recognize me…or at least he pretended he didn't. I stayed in most of the day, and Brent was so out of sorts. I finally got him to nap, and I needed fresh air. I looked out the window first and Arthur wasn't out there, so I figured it was safe." A look of sadness entered her eyes. But he had recognized me, and he came looking for me. He had some very nasty things to say about my loose morals. Then he wanted me and Brent to travel with him. According to him, I'm a great liar and could easily sell his wares." Her hands shook, and she clasped them together.

"He saw Brent and he knew. He knew he was…was his. But he thought he was born slow, and that since I was here with you I must be living in sin. Oh, Juan he only wanted me because he hated my mother. He never really wanted me. I'm a fool." She bowed her head as crimson bloomed across her cheeks. "He said I have no morals, but I told him that God forgives, and he laughed." She lifted her head and met his gaze, a small smile playing on her lips. "I was so afraid, but you came in and saved me."

"So he didn't…" He closed his eyes as heat washed over his face, then opened them again and looked into her eyes.

"No, but he planned to. He thought for sure you were spending another night out under the stars." Her mouth twisted into a wry grimace. "He's right though. I've made too many mistakes to ever claim I'm a good woman. I'm a ruined woman, who belongs in a brothel."

He handed her a clean bandana when she began to cry. He was at a loss. What was he supposed to say?

"A new start, a new husband, a new town will be just what I need," she said between sobs. "Do you believe that God forgives a person if they repent? Do you think He gives second chances?" She was biting her lip so hard he was afraid it would start to bleed.

He put his arm around her and guided her head to his shoulder. "I believe if you are truly sorrowful for what you have done and ask God's forgiveness He cleanses you of your sins. But I also believe that it—what happened with Arthur—wasn't *your* sin. You were but a child and Arthur knew what he was doing when he seduced you. You are a good, kind, loving woman, and if people can't see that then they are blind. You've managed to survive when others would have given up."

He must have said something right. She shuddered out a huge sigh, and it sounded like a sigh of contentment, and then she snuggled closer to him. He would miss her for the rest of his life. He knew it for a fact. With each lonely morning and each lonely evening, he'd wish she was at his side.

"How set are you on marry David Winstone?"

"I accepted his proposal. He's expecting me."

He was quiet for a long while. Why didn't he have enough confidence to ask her to stay? The fear of her rejection was all consuming. He didn't suggest getting some sleep, though. He wanted to hold her for as long as possible.

"What are you thinking about?" she asked.

"Not much really."

"The expressions on your face keep changing. You're thinking about the horses aren't you?"

It would be easy to say yes, but he'd been a coward for too long. "I was thinking about you." He stared straight ahead, afraid to see her face.

"I was thinking about you too. In a few years, you'll have Carlos here. You'll forget you ever met me. You'll meet a fine woman to make your wife and have a family."

"So you have my life all figured out for me, do you?" he teased as his heart squeezed in pain.

"You are the finest, most handsome man I've ever known, and I'm thankful you came into my life."

He took a deep breath. It was speak up now or never time. "Yet you want to leave me."

She pulled away and stared into his eyes. "Isn't that what we decided was for the best? You don't want me here. Your business would suffer, and I'd never forgive myself."

"I'd rather have you than more horses. But like I said before, people will buy my horses." He caressed her cheek with the back of his fingers and was rewarded when she leaned into his touch. "Tell me, Sonia, tell me your dreams."

She smiled. "No one has ever asked me what I wanted before, let alone if I even had dreams. I do have dreams, but I know they won't come true, so I'll be off tomorrow on a new adventure."

He stiffened. "Was there someone from town you had your eye on before everything happened?"

"No, nothing like that. I was a bit shy and had never even held a boy's hand before."

"I wish I was a different man. One you could be proud to have as your husband." Pain stabbed at his heart. "But I understand."

Her eyes widened and anger filled her eyes. "I've told you before Juan Settler, you being Mexican makes no difference to me. It's not even an issue, and I'd be proud to have your children."

"I don't think you really know what it would mean. You wouldn't be invited to sewing parties or asked to help out at a town picnic. I'm used to it, but you shouldn't have to suffer because of me. If we had babies, they'd be beautiful, but people wouldn't treat them the same as the other children. Kids would throw rocks at them and tell them to go back to Mexico even though they'd be born in America."

She took his hand. "Is that what happened to you?"

He nodded as painful memories constricted his chest, making it hard to breathe.

"I'm sorry people have been so cruel to you. But I don't know if you realize it…you're taking it out on me. You think the same thing will happen if you married me." She shook her head.

She didn't understand and she never would until it was too late. He'd have to let her go for her own good. "I've had a long day, and I'm exhausted."

Sonia pulled away and stood. Her eyes showed her disappointment in him, but he was doing her a favor. "Good night, Juan. Will you be here to see me off?"

"It might be easier for Brent if I make myself scarce."

"I understand. I'll see you for breakfast then. Good night." Her shoulders sagged as she walked into the bedroom.

Everything within him wanted to ask her to be his wife, but he couldn't. He wanted to, oh did he want to. Pain threatened to consume him. He needed to be up and out before she woke.

CHAPTER EIGHT

Sonia tossed and turned most of the night. She'd have circles under her eyes come morning, but it couldn't be helped. Finally, the sun started to make an appearance, its faint light filtering through the window, so she got out of bed and quickly dressed. She didn't want to miss Juan. It was going to be so very hard to say good bye to him.

Satisfied she was ready to greet the day, she walked out of the bedroom with a smile on her face. To her dismay, Juan wasn't there. He was probably in the barn, but as soon as she saw a piece of paper on the table, she knew in her heart he was gone.

Wave upon wave of heartache washed over her. She sank into the chair and reached for the note. She didn't need to read it. Her dream was over before it had begun. She read it anyway.

Sonia

It would be too hard to see you leave knowing you're going to another to be married. At least for a little while I had you and Brent in my life, and for that I'm grateful. Go, make new dreams.

Juan

New dreams...perhaps he was right, but why did it feel like her heart was being ripped out? She carefully folded the paper and put it inside her valise. Then she made breakfast for her and Brent even though she didn't have an appetite.

It was a six-hour ride to where David lived. He said he'd meet her in front of the general store. Six hours was far enough away, at least she hoped so. Brent was awake when she went into the bedroom to get him ready to go. Then she gave him breakfast. She wrapped up the biscuits to bring with them to eat along the way.

Greg hadn't said who was driving her, and she hadn't thought to ask. She set her valise and belongings on the porch and went back inside to wait for the wagon. The blocks that Juan had carved for Brent were on the floor. She swallowed back a sob as she gathered them up and went back outside to put them in the valise.

The wagon could be seen from the porch. It looked as though there was a passenger. Sonia hurried and picked up Brent and brought him outside.

"I'm going to miss you," Mercy said as she gave Sonia a hug.

"Me too. Look after Juan for me?"

"Of course. He rode off before sunrise this morning. He took enough stuff to stay away for a while. He's hurting." Mercy kissed Brent's cheek. "You be a good boy."

Brent smiled and reached for Hannah. Just then, the wagon came close enough for them to see who was in it. To Sonia's surprise it was Smitty with Scarlett at his side. Sonia wanted to groan out loud at the thought of six long hours with Scarlett. That girl hated Sonia and she hadn't been shy letting her feelings be known.

Mercy laughed. "You don't have to make a face. Scarlett is

here to show me how to make a dress. I know how to make the simplest of dresses, but I have no sense of style."

"Scarlett has a lot of style," Sonia murmured.

"She made a comment at church about my plainness, and the minister suggested she help me by teaching me." Mercy giggled. "I think it was to be her penance for saying such a thing, but I do believe I'll be the one paying the whole time."

"She's nice deep down. She just shows a selfish façade to everyone. I think she's afraid of being hurt. I knew a girl like her once. That girl was me," Sonia said.

Before Mercy could reply they could hear Scarlett complaining to her father.

"Good luck to you, Sonia," Greg said. "If you need anything, or if this David turns out to be a bad man, let us know. We'll be there to help."

Greg was the one who had thought David sounded like the best choice. Sonia furrowed her brow. "Thank you, Greg."

"Did you want me to tell Juan anything?" he asked.

"I don't know what's left to say. He thinks no woman would want him, and I don't want to ruin his dream by having his name associated with mine. You were right, Greg. It could hurt your prospects for a successful ranch."

"I'm sorry I ever said that to you, Sonia."

The wagon stopped, and Smitty climbed down and then helped Scarlett down. "All set? It'll be a long drive."

"Thank you for doing this, Smitty," Sonia said as she put her bonnet on.

"You're quite welcome. I need to check out your groom, you know."

"It's a burden, you know," Scarlett said. "But if it gets you away from the family then it's worth it."

Sonia took a step back. The sting couldn't have been worse if the girl had slapped her in the face. She turned to

Greg. "Tell Juan that my dreams were here, and I never wanted to belong to the sewing circle anyway."

Greg's brow furrowed. "I'll tell him, but he probably won't know what it means either."

But he would, Sonia knew.

After everything was loaded into the wagon, Greg helped her and Brent onto the wagon seat. Smitty flicked the lines and the horses pulled the wagon.

"I'm sorry for the way Scarlett spoke to you, Sonia. She's been particularly difficult lately. She has a good heart, I know it. I've seen it. But these last months…" Sighing, he gave a sad shake of his head.

"You don't need to apologize for her. She's trying to figure out where her life will lead her and how she'll fit in."

"I suppose you're right."

They traveled for almost three hours, sometimes in silence, sometimes making small talk. Brent grew heavy and fell asleep against her shoulder. Sonia was nodding off herself when a loud cracking noise startled the horses.

"Whoa there…" Smitty reined them in. When the wagon ground to a halt, he muttered something under his breath and jumped down. More muttering, this time some choice curses that made Sonia blush. "It's the wagon wheel. I know to always have a spare when going such a distance but I forgot. I can't believe I'd forget such a thing."

Alarm made her heart beat faster. "What can we do?"

Smitty took off his hat and ran his fingers through his hair. "The best bet is to stay right here since we have the little one with us. When we don't show up by nightfall, I'm sure David will send a telegram inquiring about you. We'll be on our way by this time tomorrow, I bet. I did pack bedrolls and food. But my head wasn't screwed on straight this morning. Last night Lynn told me that we're expecting again."

A surprise gasp escaped, and Sonia smiled, happy for the

couple. "That's exciting news and a reason to have other things on your mind instead of a wagon wheel." She handed Brent to Smitty before she climbed down. "And at least it's a pleasant day."

Smitty smiled. "That's what I like about you, Sonia. You look on the bright side of things. You've been through a lot in your young life, but you carry on making a good life for your son."

Heat began to lick at her face. "I've learned from my mistakes plus I love my son. Getting away will be best. I won't be fodder for the gossips anymore."

Sonia grabbed a blanket out of the back of the wagon and spread it out. She took Brent into her arms and sat him on it. Next she took out the blocks and put them in front of him. "We may as well have a seat."

Smitty nodded. "I'm just not used to staying put."

"Brent will keep us plenty busy."

"I'm sure he will."

JUAN WAITED in the forest until he saw the wagon go by. He thanked God when he saw it was his pa driving. Sonia was in good hands. She'd get there just fine and get married and Brent would call another man "Papa." His gut twisted.

"Come on, Journey, we might as well go home." He turned the horse around and rode to his cabin. It would feel empty without her. She hadn't spent much time in it, but he'd miss her all the same.

Juan was surprised to see Greg sitting on the cabin's steps. He slid off Journey and sat next to him. "Did something happen?"

"Scarlett came by to show Mercy about styling a dress or something. Mercy made me promise I'd be within calling distance all day. I don't want to be in my house, so here I am. I need to muck out stalls in a bit. I thought you were going to be gone for a while."

"I have horses to train before getting new ones. I just didn't want the hassle of saying goodbye."

"Sonia told me to tell you that her dreams were here and she never wanted to belong to the sewing circle anyway."

Juan closed his eyes and rode the pain out.

"Hey what's wrong? What did the message mean?"

"It means she loves me. I wish she didn't."

"You don't have feelings for her? You sure fooled me."

"Greg, I'm not good enough for her. Everyone kept saying she had the bad reputation that she wouldn't be good for me, but all that would eventually go away. But my being different, my being a Mexican? That'll never go away. I don't want it to go away. I'm proud of who I am and where I come from. But you have to admit people show their disrespect to me all the time. She's better off with that David fella."

Greg shook his head. "Juan, sometimes you have to take a chance and hope for the best. If she loves you, her marriage to someone else won't be an easy one for her."

Juan took off his hat and slapped it against his knee. "You didn't want her here, Greg. You're the one who put the idea in her head that she'd be bad for business and for me. I wish you'd never told her that. She'd been beating herself up pretty good before that."

"If I could take it back I would. I wasn't sure her feelings for you were true." He stared at the ground. "I'll admit I thought she'd be nothing but trouble. She always seemed like she was running from her situation. But since meeting that Arthur, I feel differently. The whole ride to the sheriff's office this morning he whined and complained about young girls and how they expected him to stay around after he took their virtue. The sheriff seemed to think he'd be left go in a day or so. Sonia's father saw him, so maybe he'll shoot him."

Juan grunted. If it wouldn't get him hanged, *he* would have shot the man.

"Sonia has been good for you, Juan. She makes you smile, and I think I even heard you laugh a time or two. You never really did either before, except with Carlos. Love can be found in the strangest of ways but when true love comes your way, you hold on with both hands and never let go." He chuckled. "Heck, I wasn't even sure how I felt about Mercy, but the judge insisted on marrying us to protect her from the other miners. And I love her with my whole heart. I never thought to be this happy. And with Hannah? Life is pretty near perfect." He twisted his head and pinned Juan in a meaningful stare. "I can't explain it, but my advice would be to go after her. I apologized to her for making her think she'd ruin the ranch."

Juan swallowed hard to get the lump in his throat to leave. "She feels honor bound to marry since she gave her word."

"Juan, it's not over until that ring is on her finger. Go after her and Pa."

"And when she says no? I don't think I'm that brave, Greg." Juan hung his head at his confession.

"If she says no, then you'll be in the same situation as you are now. It might hurt a bit more, but you won't have lost anything." A smile lifted his lips. "But what if she says yes?"

Mouth gaping, Juan stared at Greg. "I'd have to leave now if I'm to catch up to them. I might be too late but it's worth a try."

Greg slapped Juan on the back. "Well let's get you on your way. Journey is already all packed up. Mercy and I will be here for you no matter how it turns out."

They both stood, and Juan gave Greg a quick hug before

he bounded onto Journey. Sonia and Pa had a head start but the wagon would be traveling much slower. There was still hope.

HE RODE for a few hours and then stopped at a small stream to water Journey. He kept reminding himself that more than likely he'd be too late, but he couldn't turn around now. There was still the slightest hope she hadn't gotten to her David Winstone yet. If by some miracle he caught her in time, he was going to speak plainly so there was no mistake about what he wanted.

"Come on, Journey we need to see if we can catch up." He mounted and away they went. They had traveled for only about ten minutes when Juan spotted the wagon. It was sitting at an odd angle. He spurred Journey on and then slid down to the grassy ground.

They weren't at the wagon. He was on high alert and his stomach clenched. What had happened to them? Then he heard Brent giggling. He walked around to the other side of the wagon and he spotted them on a blanket in the shade of a tree some distance from the road having some sort of picnic.

"You scared me to death!" he called out. "I thought—well I thought something happened to you." He never took his gaze off Sonia. Her eyes widened, and she smiled at him.

"Hungry?" she asked.

He was hungry, but not for food. "What happened to the wagon?"

Smitty wiped his mouth with his napkin. "Broken wheel. I didn't put in a spare."

Juan smiled and shook his head. "Pa, *you* didn't put in a spare?"

"Had my mind on other things. But since you're here, would you mind staying with Sonia and Brent while I ride back and get a wheel?" He had the slightest of grins and there was a twinkle in his eyes.

"I suppose I could."

"Good!" he stood. "I'm going to have to borrow your horse. Now seeing it'll take me a while to get the wheel and then find another wagon, I might not be back until morning."

"Don't you worry, Pa. I have supplies to keep us comfortable for days."

"Good man. I'll be going if it's fine with you, Sonia."

"Smitty, just be careful. Juan will take good care of us." Sonia smiled.

Juan unloaded his things except for a few supplies in case his pa needed them. "You're all set."

His pa took him to the side. "I'm not sure how you feel about that little gal, but son, I wouldn't let her get away if I were you." He mounted the horse and left.

Juan stood watching for a moment, not sure of what to say to Sonia. He ended up not having to start the conversation. Brent looked up from his blocks and yelled, "Papa! Papa!"

Juan quickly walked to the blanket and scooped Brent up into his arms. He gave the boy a kiss on his cheek. "I'm so glad to you see you."

"Me too see me." Brent smiles proudly at his words.

"Come sit and have some food, Juan. You can tell me why you're here," Sonia said as she patted a place on the blanket next to her.

Juan sat down and held Brent's hands so he could stand. He had to tell her before he lost his nerve, and he had to make her listen. At least this way, she couldn't run off on him.

"Sonia, I know I've asked you to stay before, but I never gave you a very good reason—"

She waved one hand in a dismissive gesture. "I was glad to help, and you gave me shelter."

It was as though butterflies had taken over in his stomach. "If I'm going to tell you everything, I need to do it without interruption," he said softly.

Sonia nodded and worry lines etched her forehead.

"I kept telling you why you wouldn't want to stay with me, but I never told you why you should stay with me. I can provide for both you and Brent. I planned to expand the cabin. If you want, next spring you can start a vegetable garden. I'd be proud for Brent to call me Papa and to watch him grow. I'd be gone once in a while catching more horses. I won't be in your way as I'm outside a lot of the time. You already like my family and you and Mercy seem to have grown close. I'll make Brent a bed of his own. I'm a good hunter." His mind went blank. There had to be more things he could give her or do for her.

Sonia sat there silently staring at him. He should have waited. Now he had to spend probably the night with her and they weren't talking. His heart squeezed painfully. No, he refused to give up.

"Oh, heck. I'm an idiot. I still didn't give you any good reasons to stay. The real reason I want you to stay is because I love you. I love you more than I ever knew possible. You make my life complete and my heart full, both you and Brent. I want you to come back and live with me."

There, he'd said it. But she still looked doubtful…or was it disappointment on her face? "You can talk now if you want." He wanted to be sick. She would have smiled if she loved him back. "Never mind. I know what you're going to say. Just pretend this conversation never happened."

This time she seemed hurt. Brent plopped down and crawled to his mother. He climbed up her until he hung onto her shoulder. "Mama."

JUAN

Sonia's face lit up and she exuded happiness. "Did you hear what he said?" She waited until Juan nodded. "He said, Mama."

He wanted to share in her happiness, but his heart was shattered. He'd taken his chance, and it hadn't turn out the way he wished. He stood up and walked over to the wagon, pretending to look at the broken wheel. How was he going to get through until his pa came back? He hadn't felt this bad since his parents had died, and he and Carlos had nowhere to go. It had been his greatest blessing when Lynn told him she wanted to adopt both him and Carlos.

Maybe a person only got one great blessing. Dang, he'd been happy until she hid out in his cabin. He had been happy enough until he got to know her and Brent. He wanted nothing more than to go back to his cabin and lick his wounds. He wouldn't have to talk to any new women ever again.

He needed to find wood for a fire. He started to walk toward the woods.

"Juan, where are you going?"

"I need to collect wood for the fire. I'll be back." He didn't even glance at her, he just kept walking. She'd said his being Mexican didn't matter to her. Did she just say that because she knew she was leaving the next morning? He bent down and picked up a few fallen boughs. It was easy enough to say nice things when a fella didn't actually have to do them.

He made a big pile near the entrance of the woods. He'd make a couple trips bringing it near the wagon. He grabbed as much as he could carry, piled it, and went back for more. He shouldn't have come. He shouldn't have risked his heart. Why had Greg given him that message? *"Tell Juan that my dreams were here and I never wanted to belong to the sewing circle anyway."*

It had given him hope. What a fool he was. He thought it

meant she loved him. He had a hard time maintaining his usual expressionless façade. He couldn't hide from her. He'd have to keep busy and away from her until he could get ahold of himself.

After bringing all the wood he'd gathered, he went to the wagon and sorted the supplies. It didn't need doing, but he did it...and then did it again.

Finally Sonia came over and took the blocks he'd made out of her valise. She didn't say anything to him, but there was sympathy in her eyes. He was swept with a strange mixture of pride and regret. He was so glad she'd brought the blocks for Brent, but he regretted ever pouring out his feelings to her.

Taking a deep breath, he told himself to man up.

As happy as she was that Brent called her Mama, it was overshadowed by the fact that Juan only wanted her to live with him. He said he loved her, but he hadn't made one mention of marriage. He'd told her time and again he wouldn't get married. Leaving...this was her chance. David Winstone was her chance at respectability. She couldn't live with a man as a married couple if they weren't married. She'd been given a second chance by God, and she couldn't waste it. What would his parents think? In fact, it was insulting.

Why hadn't Smitty stayed while Juan went for a wheel? That would have been the proper way. But she had been able to tell Smitty thought he was matchmaking, and she'd hoped...

Somehow it hurt worse than when Arthur had slapped her. It was being told she was good enough to live with but not to give her his name... No, it was obvious. Juan knew her secrets and he felt she wasn't worthy of being a wife.

She touched her face. Was the bruise worse? She didn't have a mirror. Bruises could go either way, they could lighten or they could darken. What would her new husband think when he saw it?

Brent had fallen asleep holding one of the blocks. Sonia stood and went to the wagon. "Juan, does my bruise look worse than yesterday?"

Juan stared at her face, and he lifted his hand to touch her but dropped it again. Her heart twisted.

"It's a bit darker, I think. Does it hurt?"

"No, I guess not. I was thinking David wouldn't want to marry a bruised woman is all." No one would want to marry her. She'd be right back where she started. A single tear rolled down her face, and she turned away.

Before she knew it she was in Juan's powerful arms, laying her ear against his chest. He didn't say anything and he didn't rub his hands up and down her back like he used to. But his heart thudded heavily beneath her cheek. She swallowed hard and pushed out of his embrace.

"I should go and check on Brent." Her voice wavered.

"I can see him from here. He's fine. I need to know something. That message you told Greg to give me. Was that all pretend like your words last night?"

She furrowed her brow and scowled. "What pretend words?"

"Never mind, I'm too angry. Let's just let it be." He started to walk away but she grabbed his arm.

"I don't care how angry. I want to know what you're talking about." She put her hands on her hips.

"You said you wouldn't mind being married to a Mexican man and having his babies. And I thought the message meant you loved me. That's why I'm angry. You said nice words because you wouldn't have to make good on them since you were leaving. I just feel like a fool for coming after you."

"I meant every word."

"You love me?" His voice was full of doubt.

"Yes I do, but I refuse to live with you. It's not right."

He shook his head. "I guess you'll have to explain it to me. I don't understand."

Her chin began to quiver and she couldn't will it to stop. "You listed off your qualifications, told me you loved me and asked me to move back in with you. David wants to marry me."

Juan still appeared puzzled. "So David asking you to live with him is better than living with me? Even though we love each other."

She widened her eyes. "You never mentioned marriage, Juan. David proposed. That's the difference."

Juan immediately dropped to one knee. "Sonia, I love you with my whole heart. I never thought to find love. I never looked for it but you and Brent came along and I fell for both of you. Will you marry me?"

She stared at him.

"What?"

Tears pricked at the back of her eyes as she nodded. "Yes, Juan, I'll be happy, no I'll be overjoyed to marry you. It took you long enough to ask."

He stood and closed the distance between them. "I thought I *had* asked you. I guess I've been so nervous about coming after you."

She could feel the heat of him, and when his head lowered to kiss her, all doubt and fear magically left. Her heart felt whole again. She tilted her head back, wanting his kiss, and she didn't have to wait. The first kiss wasn't more than a brushing of his lips against hers, and she wanted to cry out in disappointment, but the second kiss lasted much longer.

He embraced her and pulled her to him. He kissed her

again then looked down at her. He caressed her cheek with the back of his hand and then he leaned down and kissed her bruise. "Yes, a man would happily marry a woman with a bruised face."

Sonia wrapped her arms around his waist and leaned against him. She was right about forgiveness and second chances. Love, excitement and something else filled her. She closed her eyes and then she felt it. It was hope. Her heart beat a bit faster but being near Juan often did that.

Pulling away, she stared at him. "I'm not dreaming, am I?"

He chuckled and kissed her forehead. "It's as real as it gets. I can get my brothers to help add to my cabin so Brent can have a room of his own."

Her face heated, and it was most certainly red. "I'm acting like a young virgin or something."

"Oh, but you might as well be. You've never been with a man who would go to the ends of the earth for you. The first time I kissed you I could tell you hadn't had any experience. The marriage bed is about showing love. So you can blush all you want. You probably don't know much. It's not a quick roll in the hay."

"How'd you know?"

"I just figured that's how it happened. You deserve to be respected as well as loved. So when do you want to get married?" He met her gaze and it humbled her to see his love shining in his eyes.

"As soon as possible. I don't want to live apart from you."

"Apart?" Juan frowned.

"I can't live with you until we're married. It wouldn't be right."

He shook his head. "So, I make my honorable intentions known, and you have to live elsewhere? I'm all for marrying the day we get to the ranch."

She laughed. "We might want it that way, but what about your ma and pa? They'll want to be there."

"As soon as Pa makes it back, we'll get a date straightened out. But it'll be in the next few days. I can't be without you longer than that."

"Mama! Papa!" She didn't think her heart could fill with more love but it did."

CHAPTER NINE

*J*uan pulled at the tie around his neck as he stood in the front of the church. What was keeping Sonia?

"I think she ran away again," Carlos announced rather loudly.

"Shh," Juan said as he elbowed Carlos in his ribs. "She will be here."

Juan looked out at the crowd in the church and wondered if they were the reason why Sonia hadn't made it down the aisle. The people that had snubbed them had suddenly had a change of heart. He knew it wasn't because of him but because of her parents and his. Somehow Sonia's story of a young pure girl who was led into sin by the peddler had melted people's hearts.

He was glad for her sake. It didn't matter to him. He just wanted to be married so he could take her home with him. It had been a long lonely week without her.

People started squirming in the pews and glancing at each other. *Had* she decided to run? No he couldn't believe that of her. Her love for him was true, as was his for her. She'd been living with his parents the last week, and he saw her at supper every night. They would later put Brent to bed together and then walk out in the moonlight. But only as far as the corral, where they could be seen.

Now the whispers had begun, and he was starting to sweat. Where was she? He met his pa's gaze and got a reassuring smile from him.

The whole family was there. Mike and Susan, Eli and Amy, Jed and Lily and his parents all sat in the front pew. His brothers and sisters sat behind them. All except for the small children. Cindy had offered to keep them at the house so they wouldn't cause a ruckus. They'd be included at the reception.

Scarlett gave him a smile that said *I told you so.* He narrowed his eyes at her, and she stopped. What was wrong with her?

Finally, Mercy hurried down the aisle with Brent in her arms and whispered into Smitty's ear. Smitty smiled, nodded to Juan and walked to the back of the church. Mercy handed Brent to Juan.

Brent smiled and crowded, "Papa!" The he kissed Juan's cheek. Juan hugged him tight.

"You look nice in your clothes."

Brent nodded. "Yes and you." He turned toward Carlos "Not you." Brent shook his head.

Carlos laughed. "Good thing I agree with you, Brent."

Suddenly all was quiet. Mercy, wearing a pink taffeta dress, walked down the aisle holding wildflowers. She'd never looked lovelier.

Juan stared at the back of the church and smiled when his pa and Sonia appeared. They started down the aisle and Juan heard the crowd gasp. Sonia looked like a fairy princess in her green lace gown. He'd never seen so many ribbons and bows and lace. It was the joy on her face that made her so very beautiful.

He couldn't take his eyes off of her. He didn't care what curves life sent him, this moment was worth it. His heart was about to explode and he hardly heard the minister. Carlos jabbed him with his elbow when Juan didn't say "I do" right away.

Juan put the ring on Sonia's finger, and they smiled into each other's eyes. Then she produced a ring and he was surprised. There wasn't a mention of a ring for him in all the planning. Delighted he waited for her to slip the ring on his finger. He barely waited for the minister to tell him he could kiss his bride.

He pulled her close with one arm and leaned down planning to give her a chaste kiss but once he got a taste of her soft lips, he deepened the kiss, until Brent squirmed. Juan drew back and kissed Brent on the cheek and so did Sonia.

Juan smiled at Carlos when he took Brent into his arms.

"May I present Mr. and Mrs. Juan Settler," the minister announced.

The applause surprised both of them as they walked arm in arm down the aisle and then climbed into a carriage rented just for the occasion. Juan heard Brent begin to cry. He jumped out, took his son from Carlos, and handed him up to Sonia before he got back in.

Never in his life had he expected to have a wife and child. He'd never imagined a woman working next to him, making their dreams come true. Most of all he'd never imagined loving a woman so very much. It never occurred to him that his heart was big enough to hold such a love. God had blessed him. He'd probably blessed him all along, but Juan had never looked for the blessings. He only saw what was wrong, not what he should be grateful for.

From now on he would look for all the many blessings each day brought.

"What are you thinking about?" Sonia asked.

"How much I love you, and what a blessing both you and Brent are."

Tears shimmered in her eyes. "You are the true blessing. You opened your heart to us and you gave the people in town a chance. Now, I do have a question for you. Do you still want to have children with me?"

Juan gazed at her and could tell his answer was of great importance. "Of course. I want to experience everything that life brings with you."

"I'm so glad the wagon wheel broke and I never made it to David Winstone. I've loved you all along, and I felt as though my heart was breaking when I left." She glanced down at herself. "So, what do you think of the dress?"

Juan laughed. "You look lovely."

"Not too many bows?"

"I'm not sure if I should answer that." He grinned.

She grinned back. "Scarlett's idea and since everyone is encouraging her to help us less stylish women, I didn't have much choice. I think she put on all the bows on purpose. I'm going to suggest she wear this dress when she weds."

That took him aback for a moment, and then he chuckled. "You're a minx. I think you look amazing with or without bows. Well, will you look at that? They all beat us to the house." Juan reached out and gave her hand a squeeze.

"I was wondering why you were driving the back road so slowly. I guess I was left out of a few of the plans."

Juan reined in the team and put on the brake. Sonia handed Brent to Mercy and waited for her husband to lift her from the carriage. *Her husband.* How many sleepless nights had she spent with her heart shattered, yearning for someone who loved her? Now her heart was about to burst but for a good reason.

She smiled into Juan's eyes as he lifted her down and then he pulled her into an embrace. "I missed you all week," he whispered into her ear. She shivered at his warm breath.

She was sorry when he let her go. Too many people wanted to congratulate them, and the next thing she knew, she was on one side of the crowd while Juan was on the other. Finally, she excused herself to go find her husband. How she love the word *husband.* A real husband. For she didn't count Roger as being a husband.

She found Juan, and he seated her at a table and went to get her a plateful of food. She twisted and turned, trying to see Brent. Finally, she saw him. He crawled over to her, grabbed her chair, pulled himself up, and laughed. She smiled back at him. Then he let go of the chair and took a few steps before falling on his backside.

"Oh my! Brent what a big boy!" She looked around and was thrilled to discover that Juan had seen it too.

When everyone had a plate filled, the minister said grace. A calming serenity came over her, and she knew they'd be just fine in their married life.

"I want to take you home," Juan whispered to her after they ate.

Her face heated and she knew it had grown bright red when Cindy giggled. Cindy had put slices of cake in front of them. She waited for Cindy to pass. "Juan, people can hear you."

"You are rather cute when you're embarrassed."

"I am not."

"Am too," Brent chimed.

"I think we need to eat our cake so we can dance," she

suggested. It took longer to get the icing wiped off of Brent than it did for him to eat it.

At last, the fiddles were being tuned and Juan stood, holding out his hand to her. Her heart beat faster as she took his hand and stood. He led her out to the area that had been roped off for dancing. His brothers and Smitty had made a real wooden one out of smooth planks Greg had gotten from a nearby mill. Smiling, Juan took her into his arms.

Her eyes widened as he led her into a waltz.

"Ma, made us learn," he whispered.

"I knew she taught you to dance, but the waltz? I'm glad."

The surprise on the guest's faces was a great sight to see. They probably thought her husband an uncultured bum. But to their credit, they'd kept any such thoughts to themselves. She hadn't heard one derogatory word or seen one slight.

The sun was going down, and the lanterns were lit. Her feet were worn out from dancing with every male there, it seemed. She sat down and watched the others dance. She also saw Juan having whiskey with his pa and brothers.

Lynn sat next to her. "We're going to take Brent for the night so you two can have a bit of privacy."

Once again Sonia felt her face heat. "Can I ask you something?"

Lynn nodded. "Of course."

"Juan said that it was supposed to be pleasurable, but I've been married before and I know how painful it is. I'm not sure what to do. I'm afraid. Is he right at all?"

A sweet smile graced Lynn's face. "I've been married twice, and each man is different in their tenderness. That's how it's supposed to be, though, sweet and tender. I think loving the man you're with will be the difference. Try to relax and just concentrate on Juan and his love. I think you'll be surprised."

Sonia stared into Lynn's eyes and was convinced she was telling the truth. "Thank you. I was so afraid."

"It's natural to be afraid when we've been abused before. Go get your husband. I'll take care of Brent."

"I want to say goodnight to Brent."

"Of course you do, but it'll only make him cry and in the end you'll give in and take him with you. He's playing with the kids, and Cindy is with him. You'll see him tomorrow. Go."

"Thank you. We'll come and get him nice and early."

"You two enjoy your morning. Don't even think about coming over until noon."

Sonia leaned over and hugged her new mother-in-law. "I'll go get Juan. Good night."

She stood and as she started to walk toward Juan, her nerves took over and she stopped and stared at him. Blood pounded in her ears. What if Lynn was wrong?

JUAN DRANK a bit of whiskey and turned his head. There stood his bride with a stricken expression on her face. What could be wrong? He handed Greg his glass and walked to her. He cupped both of her shoulders in his hands. "Sweetheart, what's wrong?"

"It's time for us to go. Lynn is keeping Brent here for the night."

He frowned. "Isn't that a good thing?"

"I'm scared." Her voice quivered.

"Brent will be just fine."

"No, I... Never mind let's go home." Her smile wasn't convincing, and Juan wondered what had happened.

They headed for the carriage, and as they started to leave, people yelled their goodbyes and well wishes. Juan smiled as he waved back, but he noticed the effort it took Sonia to wave and act happy.

He flicked the reins and drove off. Did she regret marrying him? That was all he could imagine to be wrong. His heart squeezed. Was she scared that she was stuck with him now? He dreaded arriving at his cabin. She'd tell him it was over, and she'd leave.

The cabin came into sight, and he gave her a tight smile. "I'll help you down and then take care of the horses."

This time he didn't take her into his arms; he merely held out his hand for her. He didn't understand her confusion. Heck, he didn't understand anything.

"I'll wait out here for you." She couldn't hide the fact she was shaking.

"Go on in if you like."

"Aren't you going to carry me over the threshold?"

Why was she doing this? It would be torture to hold her again. "I'll be back as soon as I can." He led the horses to the barn and unhitched them. He took his time making them comfortable and giving them extra feed. He glanced toward the house a time or two, but she still stood by the door.

Finally he had to go in. Even if it was goodbye, he'd treat her with all the love he had. He didn't want to be like Roger in any way. He walked toward the house and climbed up the steps. Her face appeared pinched in worry. He scooped her up, reached to open the door, and carried her in.

She laughed.

"I think we need to talk, Sonia." He set her on the settee and then closed the door. Feeling strangled, he then took off his tie and unbuttoned the first few buttons of his shirt so he could be comfortable.

He sat down in a chair near her. "If you want to end our marriage, please let me know now. My heart is breaking at the thought, but it's better to know than to wonder. You've been unhappy since we started to leave the reception. I'm not sure what happened, but it hurt to look at you—"

A dainty giggle stopped him.

"And now you suddenly laugh?"

She put her hand over her heart. "I never meant to worry or hurt you. You once told me that the marriage bed was a good place, but I can't help but remember the pain and the hitting. I asked Lynn, and she said it was pleasurable if you love your husband. I'm just so scared. I love you but what if I can't or if it hurts?"

He stood and went to the settee. Then he scooped her up and carried her into the bedroom and gently placed her on the bed.

"If at any time you feel uncomfortable, or if you just want to stop please tell me. I can promise there will be no hitting, and I'm hoping there won't be pain. I planned to woo you and love you and be gentle with you."

"I have a say? I-I can say stop without getting hit?"

"Sonia, have I ever hit you? Have you ever heard of me hurting a woman? You have the biggest say. We'll start with a kiss. Will that be fine with you?"

Her hand stopped shaking, but she looked doubtful.

Juan lay next to her and gave her a sweet, gentle kiss. He didn't touch her, he just kept kissing her. Finally, she wrapped her arms around his neck, and he knew they'd be just fine.

EPILOGUE

*T*hree Months Later

Juan sat on the porch steps drinking coffee and watching the sun rise. He praised God for the many blessing He'd showered on him and his family. Brent was running and talking. He'd caught up to other children his age. Sonia was with child. After not wanting a child of his own, Juan thought himself to be more excited than anyone about the baby.

Sonia slept in a bit longer these days, and Juan had gotten into a habit of drinking coffee and talking to God.

Winter would be upon them any day now, and he'd been busy preparing for a storm he was certain was coming their way. He'd tied a rope from the house to the barn so he wouldn't get lost if the wind or a total white out made it so he couldn't see. He'd also laid up extra supplies in the barn in case he got trapped there. Then he and Greg ran a line from Juan's house to Greg's house. Mostly because the women had so many what-ifs that Greg and Juan had quickly just strung it.

His brothers had helped to add to the cabin so Brent now had his own room. They'd add another come spring.

Sonia was happy, and her happiness was his happiness. Love, patience, and tenderness helped her to overcome her fears of intimacy.

The door opened behind him, and Sonia pushed him to the side so she too could enjoy her coffee and the sun. "Do you feel the chill in the air? There's that crisp smell of winter too."

"I have a feeling it's going to be a bad one."

"Brent, the baby and I have someone to help keep us warm. You give off a lot of heat at night." She smiled. "What are you feeling? Boy or girl?"

"Oh no, we're not having this conversation the whole time you're with child. I never win. If I say boy, you ask if I hate girls. If I say girl, you say I must think one boy in the family is enough."

She wrinkled her nose. "I don't do that. Do I?"

He laughed. "No of course not. I made the whole thing up," he teased.

"We can start discussing baby names. That will be fun." Her eyes twinkled.

He shook his head and laughed some more. You already have them picked out, don't you?"

She shrugged. "I have no idea what you mean."

Juan put his cup down on the porch and then did the same with hers. Then he pulled her into a loving embrace and kissed her. "I never get enough of your kisses."

"Good. That's one of the keeping warm plans I have."

THE END

I'm so pleased you chose to read Juan, and it's my sincere hope that you enjoyed the story. I would appreciate if you'd consider posting a review. This can help an author tremendously in obtaining a readership. My many thanks. ~ Kathleen

ABOUT THE AUTHOR

Sexy Cowboys and the Women Who Love Them...
Finalist in the 2012 and 2015 RONE Awards.
Top Pick, Five Star Series from the Romance Review.
Kathleen Ball writes contemporary and historical western romance with great emotion and
memorable characters. Her books are award winners and have appeared on best sellers lists including: Amazon's Best Seller's List, All Romance Ebooks, Bookstrand, Desert Breeze Publishing and Secret Cravings Publishing Best Sellers list. She is the recipient of eight Editor's Choice Awards, and The Readers' Choice Award for Ryelee's Cowboy.
Winner of the Lear diamond award Best Historical Novel- Cinders' Bride
There's something about a cowboy

facebook.com/kathleenballwesternromance
twitter.com/kballauthor
instagram.com/author_kathleenball

OTHER BOOKS BY KATHLEEN

Lasso Spring Series
Callie's Heart
Lone Star Joy
Stetson's Storm

Dawson Ranch Series
Texas Haven
Ryelee's Cowboy

Cowboy Season Series
Summer's Desire
Autumn's Hope
Winter's Embrace
Spring's Delight

Mail Order Brides of Texas
Cinder's Bride
Keegan's Bride
Shane's Bride
Tramp's Bride
Poor Boy's Christmas

Oregon Trail Dreamin'
We've Only Just Begun
A Lifetime to Share
A Love Worth Searching For

So Many Roads to Choose

The Settlers
Greg

Juan

Scarlett

Mail Order Brides of Spring Water Books 1-3
Tattered Hearts

Shattered Trust

Glory's Groom

Mail Order Brides of Spring Water Books 4-6
Battered Souls

Faltered Beginnings

Fairer Than Any

Romance on the Oregon Trail Books 1-3
Cora's Courage

Luella's Longing

Dawn's Destiny

Romance on the Oregon Trail Books 4-5
Terra's Trial

Candle Glow and Mistletoe

The Kavanagh Brothers Books 1-3
Teagan: Cowboy Strong

Quinn: Cowboy Risk

Brogan: Cowboy Pride

Sullivan: Cowboy Protector
Donnell: Cowboy Scrutiny
Murphy: Cowboy Deceived
Fitzpatrick: Cowboy Reluctant
Angus: Cowboy Bewildered
Rafferty: Cowboy Trail Boss
Shea: Cowboy Chance

The Greatest Gift
Love So Deep
Luke's Fate
Whispered Love
Love Before Midnight
I'm Forever Yours
Finn's Fortune
Glory's Groom

Made in the USA
Monee, IL
14 October 2023